Steve did something he hadn't done in twenty years of law enforcement: lowered his weapon in shock.

"Rosalyn?"

She reached up and lowered the hood of her windbreaker as she turned completely around.

It was her. Beautiful black hair, gorgeous blue eyes. Even the splattering of freckles over her nose. Rosalyn was alive.

Which was impossible because he'd just ID'd her dead body a few hours ago. Steve didn't care. By whatever miracle she was here—and he would get her to explain it all, no doubt—he would take it.

He holstered his weapon and pulled her into his arms. Then yanked her back immediately, looking closer at the rest of her body.

Rosalyn was here. She was alive.

And unless he was very, very wrong, she was definitely pregnant.

BATTLE TESTED

JANIE CROUCH

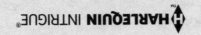

HARLEQUIN INTRIGUE®

This book is dedicated to my aunt Donna. You are a blessing to me and so many others. Thank you for all the times you brushed my hair (because goodness knows I didn't do it) and loved me like a second mother. And for teaching me that romance books are the best books.

ISBN-13: 978-1-335-72074-0

Battle Tested

Copyright © 2016 by Janie Crouch

This edition published by arrangement with Harlequin Books S.A.

For questions and comments about the quality of this book, please contact us at CustomerService@Harlequin.com.

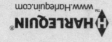 HARLEQUIN®™

Printed in U.S.A.

www.Harlequin.com

Recycling programs for this product may not exist in your area.

Janie Crouch has loved to read romance her whole life. The award-winning author cut her teeth on Harlequin Romance novels as a preteen, then moved on to a passion for romantic suspense as an adult. Janie lives with her husband and four children overseas. She enjoys traveling, long-distance running, movie watching, knitting and adventure/obstacle racing. You can find out more about her at janiecrouch.com.

CAST OF CHARACTERS

Steve Brackett—Director of Omega Sector's Critical Response Division.

Rosalyn Mellinger—On the run from a stalker; has been moving from state to state for months trying to get rid of him.

Brandon Han—Brilliant profiler for Omega Sector; engaged to Andrea Gordon.

Liam Goetz—SWAT team member and hostage rescue expert.

Jon Hatton—Profiler and crisis management expert.

Andrea Gordon—Naturally gifted behavioral analyst; engaged to Brandon Han.

Derek Waterman—SWAT team leader; married to Molly Humphries-Waterman.

Lillian Muir—SWAT team member and helicopter pilot.

Molly Humphries-Waterman—Crime lab director at Omega; married to Derek Waterman.

Joe Matarazzo—Billionaire and hostage negotiator for Omega.

Ashton Fitzgerald—SWAT team member and sharpshooter expert.

Donny Showalter—Civilian trapped in a madman's deadly game.

Chapter One

Rosalyn Mellinger had reached her breaking point.

She was exhausted, frightened and about to run out of money.

Sitting in a diner in Pensacola, Florida, one she'd chosen because she could see both the front customer door and the rear employee entrance from her corner booth, she huddled around the third cup of coffee she'd had with her meager meal, stretching out her stay here as long as possible.

Although sitting with her back to the wall didn't help when she had no idea what the person who stalked her looked like. She tensed every time the tiny bell chimed signaling someone new had come through the door, like it had just now.

The couple in their mid-eighties, entering and shuffling slowly to a table, were definitely not the Watcher.

But she knew he was around. She knew because she would get a note later tonight—or an email or a text or a phone call—that would say something about her meal here. About what she'd eaten or the name of her waitress or how she'd used sweetener in her coffee rather than sugar.

Some sort of frightening detail that let her know the Watcher had been nearby. Just like he had been for the last five months. She scanned faces of other patrons to see who might be studying her but couldn't find anyone who looked like they were paying her any attention.

It always seemed to be that way. But still the Watcher would know details as if he had been sitting here at the booth with Rosalyn. And would mention the details in a message to her, usually a note slid under her door in the middle of the night.

Rosalyn clutched her coffee cup, trying to get her breathing under control.

Or maybe the Watcher wouldn't say anything about the diner at all. Maybe he wouldn't contact her for days. That happened sometimes too. Rosalyn never knew what to expect and it kept her on the precipice of hysteria.

All she knew for certain was the constant acid of fear burning in her gut.

Her waitress, Jessie, who couldn't have been more than eighteen or nineteen years old, wiped the table next to Rosalyn's, then came to stand by her booth. The kid looked decidedly uncomfortable.

"I'm sorry, ma'am, but my manager said I would have to ask you to leave if you're not going to order anything else. The dinner crowd is coming in."

The burn in Rosalyn's belly grew at the thought of leaving the diner, although she didn't know why. She was no safer from the Watcher in here than she was somewhere else.

He'd found her again last night. Rosalyn had been in Pensacola for four days, staying at a different run-down hotel each night. Three nights had passed with no message, no notes, and she'd let just the slightest bit of hope enter her heart that she had lost the Watcher permanently.

Heaven knew she had driven around enough times to get rid of anyone who followed. Hours' worth of circles and sudden turns around town to lose any tails. Then she had parked at a hotel before sneaking across strip malls and a small park to *another* hotel about a mile away just in case there was some sort of tracker on her car. It seemed to have worked for three nights.

Rosalyn thought maybe she had figured it out. That the Watcher had been tracking her car and that's how he always found her. She would gladly leave the car rotting in the wrong hotel parking lot if it meant she could get away from the man who stalked her.

But then last night a note had been slipped under the hotel door as she slept.

When she saw the envelope lying so deceptively innocently on the floor of her hotel by the door as she woke up this morning, she promptly vomited into the trash can by the bed.

She finally found the strength to get up and open the unsealed envelope and read the note. Handwritten, like them all.

Sorry I haven't been around for a few days. I know you must have missed me. I missed you.

She almost vomited again, but there was nothing left in her stomach.

She took the note and put it in the cardboard box

where she kept all the other notes. Then she meticulously put the box back inside her large duffel bag. From her smaller tote bag, the one she always kept with her, she took out her notebook. With shaky hands she logged the date and time she found the note, and its contents.

She'd taken her bags and gone back to her car—a tracker there obviously wasn't the problem—and driven toward the beach and ended up at this diner. She needed to get on the move again. But she didn't know how—her savings from when she'd had a decent-paying job as an accountant were gone. And she didn't know where she would go even if she had had money.

The Watcher found her no matter where she went.

Sometimes she was convinced he was in her head since he seemed to know everything she did and thought. But that would mean she was crazy.

An idea that was becoming more and more acceptable.

Rosalyn rubbed her eyes. Exhaustion weighed every muscle in her body.

"Ma'am?"

None of this was her waitress's fault. She turned to the girl, who seemed so much younger even though she was probably only five or six years less than Rosalyn's twenty-four. "Of course. I'm sorry, Jessie. Just let me pay my bill and get my stuff together."

Jessie shuffled her feet. "No need to pay anything. I already took care of that for you. Pay it forward and all that."

Rosalyn wanted to argue. Jessie had been working hard the three hours Rosalyn had been in the booth.

The girl was probably saving up for college and needed the money.

But the truth was, Rosalyn was down to her last twenty dollars. Not having to pay six dollars for her meal would help a lot.

Being able to live a normal life and return to a regular job would help a lot more, but Jessie's gesture was still touching.

"Thank you," Rosalyn whispered to the girl. "I truly appreciate it."

"I can probably hold my manager off for another thirty minutes if that will help you. I'm sorry I can't do more."

"No. I'll be fine. Thanks."

The girl nodded and walked away.

Rosalyn wondered if she would read about her conversation with Jessie later tonight in the note the Watcher left her. Or even worse, if Jessie would end up dead. That had happened three months ago with the detective in Shreveport, Louisiana, when she'd passed through. Rosalyn had taken a chance and told him what was happening and found, to her surprise, that he believed her. Detective Johnson was the one who suggested she keep all the notes and take photos of any texts and try to record any phone messages. He was the one who got her the notebook and told her to write down everything that happened.

The relief to find someone who believed her, who didn't think she was just out for attention like her family had, was overwhelming. Finally the feeling of not being utterly alone.

Unfortunately, Detective Johnson—a healthy fifty-

year-old man—suddenly died of a heart attack two
days after meeting with Rosalyn. He was found in his
bed. Natural causes, the newspaper said. Rosalyn was
heartbroken that she'd so unfortunately lost the one
person who had listened and believed her.

Until she received an anonymous email the next day
with a link to a drug called succinylcholine. A drug
that in a large enough dose caused heart attacks but
was virtually untraceable in a victim's system.

Detective Johnson's death had been no accident.

Neither had the mechanic's—a man named Shawn
who had been super nice and repaired Rosalyn's car
at a deeply discounted rate a month ago in Memphis.
She mentioned to him that she was on the run. Didn't
want to say more than that, but he asked. Shawn's sister had an ex who had turned violent and terrorized
her. Shawn recognized some of the same symptoms
in Rosalyn. He pressed and Rosalyn gave him some
details. Not all of them, but enough. He invited her to
his mother's house for dinner, explaining the importance of not going through something like this alone.

Rosalyn, almost desperate for a friend, agreed.
When she came back to the shop that night, she found
the place surrounded by cops.

Shawn had been a victim of a "random act of violence" as he was closing up his garage. He was dead.

She still had the newspaper clipping that had been
slipped under her door the next morning.

Rosalyn rubbed her stomach against the burn. She
hadn't spoken to a single person about the Watcher
since that day. She'd just kept on the run, trying to
stay ahead of him.

He'd found her again. Pensacola was the sixth town she'd moved to in five months. He always found her. She wasn't sure how.

Exhaustion flooded her as she grabbed her tote bag and walked toward the door. Jessie gave her a small wave from behind the servers' station and Rosalyn smiled as best she could. She was almost to the entrance when she stopped and turned around, walking back to Jessie.

The girl looked concerned. For Rosalyn or *because* of her, Rosalyn couldn't tell. Rosalyn took six dollars out of her bag.

"Here." She handed the money to Jessie. "Paying for my meal was very kind and I'm sure it will get you karma points. But I know you're working hard, so I'll pay for my own meal."

"Are you sure?"

No, she wasn't sure. All she knew was that she couldn't take a chance that something would happen to this pretty young woman because she'd spotted Rosalyn six dollars' worth of salad and chicken.

"Yes." She pressed the money into Jessie's hand. "Thanks again, though."

Rosalyn turned and walked out the door feeling more lonely than she had in…ever.

She couldn't do this anymore.

What good was it to run if the Watcher was just going to find her again? What good did it do to talk to people if any ties she made were just going to get them hurt?

And at what point would the Watcher stop toying with her and just finish her off? Rosalyn had no doubt her death was his endgame. She just didn't know when or how.

Maybe she should just save him the trouble and do it herself. At least then she would have some measure of control.

She looked down the block toward the beach. She would go sit there. Think things through. Try to figure out a plan.

Even if that plan meant taking her own life. That had to be better than allowing innocent people to die because of her. Or living in constant fear with no end in sight.

She began walking toward the beach. She would sit on the sand, watch the sunset. Because damn it, if this was going to be her last day on earth—either by her own hand or the Watcher's—she wanted to feel the sun on her face one last time.

Beyond that, she had no idea what to do.

Chapter Two

Steve Drackett, director of the Omega Sector Critical Response Division, was doing nothing. He couldn't remember the last time that had happened.

And even more so, he was doing nothing in a tiki-themed bar on the Florida Panhandle. In *flip-flops*.

He was damn certain that had *never* happened.

It was his first real vacation in ten years. After his wife died twelve years ago, there hadn't been much point in them. Then he'd become director of the Critical Response Division of Omega—an elite law enforcement agency made up of the best agents the country had to offer—and there hadn't been time.

But here he was on the Florida Panhandle, two days into a weeklong vacation for which his team had pitched in and gotten for him. Celebrating his twenty years of being in law enforcement.

And to provide him with a little R & R after he was almost blown up last month by a psychopath intent on burning everything and everyone around her.

Either way, he'd take it. Home in Colorado Springs could still be pretty cold, even in May. Pensacola was already edging toward hot. Thus the flip-flops.

Steve sat at the far end of the bar, back to the wall, where he had a nice view of both the baseball game on TV and the sunset over the ocean, along with an early-evening thundershower that was coming in, through the windows at the front of the bar. It also gave him direct line of sight of the entrance, probably not necessary here but an occupational hazard nonetheless.

The cold beer in his hands and an order of wings next to him on the bar had Steve just about remembering how to unwind. Nothing here demanded his attention. The bar was beginning to fill up but everyone seemed relaxed for the most part. The hum of voices, laughter, glasses clinking was enjoyable.

As someone whose job on most days was literally saving the world, the tiki bar was a nice change.

Then the woman walked through the door.

He glanced at her—as did just about every pair of male eyes in the bar—when she rushed in trying to get out of the sudden Florida storm. Another couple entered right behind her for the same reason, but Steve paid them little attention.

She was small. Maybe five-four to his six-one. Wavy black hair that fell well past her shoulders. Slender to the point of being too skinny. Mid-twenties.

Gorgeous.

Steve forced his eyes away, although his body stayed attuned to her.

She didn't belong here—he had already summed that up in just a few moments. Not here in a tiki bar where the patrons were either on vacation or trying to just relax on a Sunday evening.

She wasn't wearing some flirty skirt or shorts and

tank top or any of the modes of dress that bespoke enjoying herself on a Florida beach in mid-May. Not that there was anything wrong with how she was dressed: khaki pants and a blue button-down shirt. No flip-flops for this black-haired beauty, or any other type of sandals. Instead she wore athletic shoes. Plain. White.

Her bag was also too large for a casual outing or catching a couple of beers for an hour or two. And clutched too tightly to her.

This woman looked ready to run. From what or to what, Steve had no idea.

Steve had been out of active agent duty for the last ten years. His job now was behind a desk on most days. A big desk, an important one. But a desk nonetheless. He didn't need to be an agent in the field to know the most important thing about the woman who'd just walked into the bar: she was trouble.

Since trouble was the very thing he was trying to get away from here in flip-flop Florida, Steve turned back to his beer and wings. Back to the game.

But as he finished his food, he found his eyes floating back to her.

She was obviously over twenty-one, so it was legal for her to be here. If she wanted to take off in a hurry—with her oversize tote-type bag—as long as she wasn't doing anything illegal, it was her own business.

She didn't want to buy a drink—he noticed that first. But as the storm lingered, then grew worse, she obviously knew she'd have to or else go back out in it. She ordered a soda.

She sat with her back to the wall.

She tried not to draw attention to herself in any way.

She was scared.

Steve finished one beer and started another. He flexed his flip-flop-enclosed toes.

Not his monkeys. Not his circus.

This woman was not his problem, but he still couldn't stop glancing her way every once in a while. She barely moved. Unfortunately, Steve wasn't the only one whose attention she had caught. Just about every guy in the place was aware of her presence.

At first men waited and watched. Was she meeting someone? A husband? Boyfriend? When it became obvious she wasn't, they slowly began circling. Maybe not literally but definitely in their minds.

Then some began circling literally.

A couple of local boys who had been here since before Steve arrived—and had been tossing beers back the whole time—worked their nerve up to go sit next to the woman. She didn't give much indication that she was interested, but that didn't deter them.

Since the baseball game was over, someone turned on the jukebox and a few couples were dancing to some Jimmy Buffett song. One of the guys stood and asked the woman to dance but she shook her head no. He reached down and grabbed her hands and tried to pull her to a standing position, obviously thinking she was playing hard to get.

Steve could read her tension from all the way across the bar, but the guys talking to her obviously couldn't.

He should leave now. He knew he should just walk away. The boys weren't going to get too out of hand. As soon as the woman put them down hard, they would leave her alone.

She was trouble. He knew it. He should go.

He sighed as he put money on the bar for his meal and began to walk toward the woman and the two men who were now both trying to get her to dance. He hadn't become the director of one of the most elite law enforcement groups in the country by walking away from trouble.

He stepped close to the first local guy, deliberately invading his space. The way the guy was invading the woman's.

"Excuse me, fellas. The lady doesn't want to dance."

"How do you know?" The other guy snickered. "Are you her dad?"

The woman's eyes—a beautiful shade of blue that stood out in sharp juxtaposition against her dark hair—flew to Steve's. She winced in apology at the crack about his age.

Steve was probably fifteen years older than the woman. Not quite old enough to be her father, but probably too old to be anything else to her.

"No, not her father. Just someone old enough and sober enough to realize when a woman is uncomfortable."

"She's not—" The guy stopped and really looked at the woman then—the way she was clutching her bag, discomfiture clear on her face.

"The lady doesn't want to dance," Steve said again.

The local guy and his buddy released the woman, murmuring apologies. Steve stepped back relieved he wasn't going to have to make some show of strength. He could've. Could've had both men unconscious on the ground before they were even aware what sort of trouble they were facing. But the guys hadn't meant any harm.

Steve nodded at the woman as the locals walked away. He didn't step any closer or try to talk to her. His flirting skills were rusty at best and this lady obviously wasn't here to scope out men. Steve turned to make his way back to his seat only to find someone had already taken his place.

Looked like it was time to go.

That was fine. It wasn't like Steve had any grand plans for his evening here in the tiki bar. He began walking toward the door.

"Thank you."

He heard her soft voice as the black-haired beauty's hand touched his arm. Steve stopped and turned toward her.

He smiled. It felt a little unpracticed. "I don't think they meant any harm, but it was no problem."

"There was a time I would've let them both have it, but I just don't seem to have it in me lately." She looked a little surprised that she was even talking to him.

She was skittish, scared. She'd been that way since the moment she'd walked in. It made him want to wrap an arm around her, pull her close and tell her to take a breath. He'd protect her from whatever demons she was trying to fight.

It surprised him a little that he felt that way. His entire life had been spent helping people, first as an FBI agent, then as he was recruited into Omega Sector. But usually he was more at a distance, less personal.

He already felt personal with this woman and he didn't even know her name.

"I'm sure you could've handled them. I just was doing my fatherly duty."

She snorted and humor lit her blue eyes. "Father, my ass. You're what? Thirty-nine? Forty?"

"Forty-one."

"Oh. Well, he should've said *grandfather*, then."

Her smile was breathtaking. Steve couldn't stop himself from taking a step toward her. "I'm Steve Drackett."

She shook his outstretched hand. He knew the thought that a flash of heat hit them both as their skin touched was both melodramatic and sentimental. Steve was neither of those things.

But he still felt the heat.

"I'm Rosalyn."

No last name. He didn't press. It was just another sign she was trouble, but Steve somehow couldn't bring himself to care.

"Can an old man buy you a drink or something?"

She studied him hard as they finally released hands. They were halfway between the bar and the door. He honestly wasn't sure which way she'd choose. To stay with him or to leave.

She ended up choosing both.

"May I ask you something?" She slid her tote more fully onto her shoulder. She had to step a little closer so they could hear each other over the noise in the bar. He found himself thankful for the chaos around them.

"Sure."

"Are you some sort of psycho? A killer or deranged stalker or both?"

She asked the question so seriously Steve couldn't

help but laugh. "Nope. Scout's honor." He held up his hand in what he was sure was an incorrect Scout salute. "I'm an upstanding member of society. Although you know if I was a crazy killer, I probably wouldn't answer that question honestly."

She shrugged, her eyes back to being haunted. "I know. I guess I just wanted you to tell me so I could see if I would believe you."

"Do you?"

She smiled so sadly it damn near broke his heart. "I think so. Or maybe I just don't care anymore. And to answer your question, yes, you can buy me a drink. But let's get out of here."

Chapter Three

Rosalyn knew her actions bordered on reckless. Even if she hadn't known she had a deranged stalker following her every move, leaving a bar with a man she'd just met would still have been pretty stupid.

He'd laughed—in a kind way, but still obviously thinking she was joking—when she'd asked if he was a killer or crazy. But like he'd said, no true villain would give her an honest answer about that.

Actually, she believed the Watcher would. If she ever met him face-to-face and asked him outright if he was her stalker, she believed he might actually tell her.

Steve Drackett wasn't the Watcher. He might be an ordinary garden-variety psycho, but he wasn't the psycho she was desperately attempting to escape right now.

And in that case, she was willing to take her chances with him.

She looked up at him as he led her to the door. He had joked about being a grandpa but that couldn't have been further from the truth. His brown hair might be graying just the slightest bit at the temples, but that was the only sign whatsoever that he wasn't a man fifteen years younger. His green eyes seemed kind, at least to her, but the rest of his face was hard and unforgiving. Stark cheekbones, strong chin. Definitely not a pretty face but very much a handsome one.

His body was well honed—the black T-shirt Steve wore left no doubt he was in excellent physical shape. His khaki shorts were quite appropriate for a bar in Florida on a May evening, but she doubted it was what he normally wore. She was positive the flip-flops weren't.

"If you're not a psychopath, what do you do, Steve?" she asked as they walked out the door. Humid air from the coast blasted them. The storm had moved out to sea, but dampness still hovered everywhere, a sure sign another storm would be coming.

"Present occupation is beach bum. I'm here on vacation from Colorado."

They walked down the steps. "Mountains. Nice. I've never been there. Are you a bum there, too?"

He hesitated slightly before he smiled. "Worse. Management."

He didn't want to tell her what he did for a living. Okay, fair enough. She hadn't told him her last name.

Of course, she was doing it for his own safety.

"Are you from around here?" Steve asked. "Do you have a bar you'd suggest?"

She didn't want to go to a bar. Not somewhere the Watcher could hear them, see them.

"How about a six-pack and walk on the beach?"

He smiled down at her. "That might break some open-beverage-container laws, but I'm willing to risk it."

Rosalyn didn't know exactly what she'd been expecting when she'd left the bar with Steve, but the next few hours were not it.

They bought their beers and sat alone, where no one—not even the Watcher—could possibly hear them.

And they talked. About everything and nothing.

He told her about his wife—his high school sweetheart—who had died in a car accident twelve years ago. About places he'd traveled. Even a little bit about his job, that he was a manager in some sort of division office and how he sometimes felt more like he was babysitting than anything else.

Rosalyn was vague without being dishonest. She told him she had a mother and sister but wasn't close to either—an understatement. She told him a little about her college years and her job as an accountant. When he made a joke about the size of her bag, she told him she never went anywhere without it. Told him she was taking some time off, traveling around a little bit, trying to "find herself."

She somehow managed not to laugh hysterically as she said it.

Steve was a good listener, a friendly talker. He never made a move on her or made her feel uncomfortable. He seemed to be both completely at ease but at the same time completely surprised at their continued, comfortable conversation.

He obviously didn't spend a lot of time picking up strangers at a bar.

At some point deep in the night—it had to have been nearly four o'clock but Rosalyn wasn't sure—it began to rain again, gently, but enough that they couldn't stay here on the beach any longer.

It looked like her reprieve was over. She needed to make her way back to her car. Maybe she'd catch a couple hours of sleep in it—the thought of being out in the open like that made her skin crawl, but what choice did she have? She was out of money. A hotel, even a cheap one, was no longer an option.

She stood and Steve got up beside her, helping her. She smiled at him. "Thanks for hanging with me. It was nice to have a peaceful night."

"Been a long time since you had one?"

She was tempted to tell him about the Watcher. To share while they had complete privacy. But knew she couldn't. Some middle-management guy from some business in Colorado couldn't remedy this situation.

"Seems like it," she said instead.

"Anything I can help with?"

She looked up at him. He was a nice guy. A nice, hot, utterly delectable guy. For the hundredth time that evening she wished she had met Steve under different circumstances.

"I'm fine. But thank you for asking." She smiled, trying to make it as authentic as possible. Trying not to think about the darkness that hovered all around them that she would have to face alone in just a few minutes.

As if the weather could hear her thoughts, it started raining a little harder.

He touched her gently near her elbow. "I need to tell you something I probably should've mentioned earlier but couldn't figure out how to do it without coming across like a jerk."

She braced herself for bad news. "Okay."

"My beach bungalow is about two hundred yards

that way." He pointed up the beach. "It's a ridiculous room. Some sort of romance package. My colleagues at work chipped in and got it for me."

She didn't know what she'd expected him to say, but that wasn't it. "Oh."

"You're welcome to come in. Get out of the rain. No expectations or anything like that." He shrugged, the awkwardness on his tense face adorable. He obviously didn't want her to feel pressured. "The peaceful night doesn't have to end right now."

Rosalyn looked out at the darkness again. She knew what waited for her there. Fear. Isolation. Panic.

Steve reached up and tucked a damp strand of her hair behind her ear. He didn't say anything. Didn't try to talk her into it or put pressure on her in any way. Just stood silently, letting her know he was there if she wanted to go with him but he was fine if she didn't.

The lack of pressure, more than anything, helped her make the decision.

"Okay, just for tonight."

She couldn't take a chance and let the Watcher find her again. Find Steve.

He smiled and took her hand. They began to run through the sand toward his room. Like he'd said, it wasn't far.

The oceanside bungalow was nice inside: sort of what one would expect for the romance package on the beach. A king-size bed with a teal bedspread and canopy roof. A couch and chair over in the reading-nook section.

And a huge heart-shaped Jacuzzi tub in the far corner.

Rosalyn looked over at Steve, who grinned sheepishly.

"You failed to mention the giant heart-shaped Jacuzzi in the middle of your room."

Steve laughed. "I wasn't sure if it would work in my favor or against me."

"Are you sure you weren't supposed to be on your honeymoon here or something?"

Steve laughed again, crossing to the bathroom to grab them both a towel to dry off from the rain. Rosalyn set her tote bag down on the chair in the sitting area.

"Honestly, I just booked a normal room in the hotel section. When I got here, I found out I had gotten an upgrade—thanks to my colleagues chipping in. I'm sure they scoped out pictures and knew exactly what they were getting for me. Including the huge roll of condoms." He rolled his eyes, gesturing to the sparkling box on the nightstand. Rosalyn couldn't help but laugh.

"It's nice that they like you so much."

Steve shrugged. "They like to get rid of me for a week, that's for sure. And a not-so-subtle hint to come back more relaxed."

She had no doubt Steve was well respected, a good man. Guilt over the danger she was putting him in washed over her.

"Hey, what's going on?" He saw her face and walked over so he was standing in front of her. He put his thumb under her chin when she wouldn't look at him. "Do you regret coming here? Feel uncomfortable? If so, I can give you a ride wherever you need to go."

She didn't regret coming. She wanted to stay. Wanted more than just the safe haven Steve was offering.

She wanted him.

He looked so big standing in front of her. So able to take care of himself. Not someone who could be taken by surprise by someone else.

But she knew the Watcher didn't play fair. He'd taught her that.

"No, I'm not uncomfortable with you. The opposite, in fact. I just—" She stopped, not knowing what to say. She couldn't explain. Couldn't take the chance.

"What?" he asked gently.

"It's not good for you to be here with me, Steve. I'm afraid I'll only bring heartache for you." Or worse.

"Are you married?" he asked.

"No." She shook her head. "Never have been."

He took a step closer. She could smell his damp skin, the saltiness of the sea air and something that was distinctly male. She breathed in deeply.

"Are you running from the law?"

"No," she whispered as he moved closer again, his body now so close to hers she could feel the heat. She leaned closer, unable to stop herself.

"Then I don't think there's any reason at all for you to leave this room if you don't want to."

His lips closed the inches between them and she couldn't think of any response even if there'd been a good one anyway. Instead she just gave herself over to the kiss.

If she was going to lose everything, she was going to have this one night with this gorgeous, strong man first. Tomorrow be damned.

The heat all but consumed them both. Her arms reached up to wrap around his shoulders, then his neck. She clutched at his hair, too impassioned to be gentle.

Steve didn't mind at all. His arms circled her waist, then reached lower to cup her hips and pull her up and into him.

Both of them gasped.

He took possession of her mouth. There was no other word for it. *Possession.* His tongue stroked against hers and fire licked at them both. Her fingers linked behind his neck to capture him. Not that he seemed interested in being anywhere but pressed up against her.

"Rosalyn." Her name was reverent on his lips.

She began walking forward, causing him to move backward toward the bed. His arms were still wrapped around her hips making sure they were fully pressed together. When his knees finally hit the bed and he fell backward, he lifted her—as if she weighed nothing at all—and pulled her on top of him.

"Are you sure this is what you want?" he murmured. "It's still okay if you just want to be here. Nothing has to happen."

He would say that while she was lying flat on top of him? They weren't undressed yet, but Rosalyn had no doubt they would be soon. In her experience most guys would call her a tease—or much worse—if she decided to call a halt to everything at this point.

"You would stop now if I asked you to?"

He threaded his hands in her hair and pulled her back so he could see her more clearly.

"Of course. Is that what you want?"

"No. Just most guys would give a woman a hard time if she decided to change her mind now."

"Honey, a real man accepts that a woman can change

her mind at any time and respects the word *no* if he hears it."

Was it possible to fall a little bit in love with someone you'd known for only a few hours?

Rosalyn sat up, her legs straddling Steve's hips. She unbuttoned her shirt and slowly peeled it over her shoulders. "Well, thanks for asking, but I have no desire to stop." She pulled her sneakers and socks off and threw them over the side of the bed.

Steve crossed his arms under his head and just watched her. "Thank goodness. I would've stopped, but I sure as hell didn't want to."

She gasped as he sat up suddenly, forcing them even closer together. He spun and scooted them farther on the bed before dropping her down so he was now on top. She helped him discard his shirt, then pulled him back down to her.

His lips met hers again. No, she wasn't interested in stopping. She was already coming apart inside. She held on to Steve and let his lovemaking chase away the demons that weren't far outside the door.

THEY DIDN'T LEAVE the bungalow the entire next day, which was fine with Rosalyn. Who needed the beach? Especially on a cloudy, dreary day. Instead they made use of the bed and the couch and very good use of the heart-shaped hot tub. Steve ordered room service for every meal.

Steve's colleagues might have meant the room as a joke—and heaven knew it wasn't tasteful in its decorating—but Rosalyn loved every bit of it.

It was her own hideaway. The Watcher obviously

didn't know she was here. And as long as she stayed inside, there was no way he would find her.

She wondered if she could talk Steve into staying in the room forever. She looked over at him sleeping in the bed next to her right now, so late at night. His sexy face relaxed in sleep. It hadn't always been that way. She'd seen his face tensed in passion or smiling as he talked to her and told her a story from his past. She'd also seen the concern when she caught him studying her when he thought she wasn't paying attention.

He was worried about her.

If he knew about the Watcher, he'd be less concerned about her well-being and more concerned with his own. Might even ask her to leave right away.

Every person she'd told about the Watcher who believed her had wound up dead. She wouldn't take that chance with Steve. She'd just live in this little bungalow of fantasy until it didn't exist anymore. Then she would go.

But she knew she'd be leaving a little part of her heart behind when she did. She rolled onto her side so she could study him more fully. She reached out and stroked his hair by his ear, drawing her fingers down his cheek. He turned his face toward her, seeking her touch even in his sleep.

She should sleep now too. It had been a pleasurable but exhausting day and now it was late. Who knew what tomorrow would bring.

Her eyes were drifting closed when she heard the sound.

It didn't wake Steve. Why would it? It was just the barest whisper of a noise. If her body and mind hadn't already been programmed to listen for it—to fear it above all else—Rosalyn wouldn't have heard it either.

The sound of an envelope being slid under the door.

Her heart stopped and her breathing became ragged. The acid that burned in her stomach—blessedly missing for the last day—returned with a force that caused Rosalyn to ball up on the bed.

She bit her fist, tears streaming down her face. She didn't want to awaken Steve. If she did, she'd never be able to keep this a secret from him.

The Watcher had found her again.

Rosalyn lay on the bed for what seemed like forever trying to get herself under control. She finally managed to crawl off, dropping silently to the floor, and stumbled over to where the envelope lay.

With shaking hands she picked it up and pulled out the paper from inside.

If you like Steve so much, I guess I'll need to meet him soon.

She swallowed the sob in her throat. No. She couldn't allow the Watcher to come after Steve. The thought galvanized her into action.

Within minutes she had silently dressed and grabbed her bag. Steve had rolled over toward her side of the bed, as if he was seeking her missing form, but Rosalyn refused to let herself think about it. If she did, she would never make it out.

And she had to concentrate on where she was going to go. The time with Steve had given her the strength not to give up her battle against the Watcher. To keep fighting. But it hadn't given her a course of action with which to do that. She didn't have any money and she had no plan.

She spotted Steve's wallet on the dresser. He'd used it each time he'd paid for the food that had been delivered. Food he wouldn't even consider letting her help pay for—good, considering how broke she was.

Shame beat down on Rosalyn as she opened his wallet and took out the cash. One hundred and eighty-three dollars.

She didn't know how far it would get her, but at least it would get her away from here. Get the Watcher away from Steve.

She looked down at his naked back, his hips and legs tangled in the sheets. He'd never know how much he'd meant to her. What he'd given her in a time she'd needed so much.

He'd just remember her as a one-and-a-half-night stand and the woman who stole his cash. She'd become a cocktail story for him. A joking warning to his friends.

The tears leaked out of her eyes. This time she didn't even try to stop them.

Thinking about her would be distasteful for Steve.

But at least he would be alive.

Chapter Four

Six months later

"Would it be okay for us to see Steve now or should we make an appointment?" Brandon Han, Omega's top profiler, asked one of Steve's assistants in the outer office.

"Yeah, maybe we should make an appointment. For around eighteen months from now." That was Liam Goetz, leader of the hostage rescue team. "When hopefully Steve is in a better mood."

Cynthia, the assistant who kept his entire office running, laughed. "I think it's safe now."

Steve winced. Obviously nobody realized the door to his office was cracked and he could hear everything they were saying.

"Should we remove our weapons?" Liam asked.

"Why? Are you afraid you might shoot him?" Cynthia's gentle laughter didn't make Steve feel better.

"Are you kidding? I'm afraid he might take them and shoot *us*."

The topic moved on to more neutral ground: Liam's

twins and Tallinn, the little girl he and his wife had adopted. Liam had pictures. Steve stopped listening.

Liam's jokes didn't bother him—Liam was always making jokes—but Brandon's initial question did. These men were an important part of the Critical Response Division's inner team. Steve's team. Moreover, they were his friends. They didn't need an appointment to see him.

But evidently they thought so given Steve's behavior over the last few months.

Rosalyn.

He ran a hand over his eyes, then turned his chair so he was facing the Rocky Mountains out the window.

When he'd awakened as the sun began to rise in Pensacola and found her gone, he'd at first thought she'd decided to walk on the beach or run out to get donuts or something. Heaven knew they hadn't left the room in a day and a half. Maybe she'd needed some air.

Then he realized all her stuff, including that giant catchall bag she carried, was gone.

Going against his nature, Steve still gave her the benefit of the doubt. She was scared of something, he knew. He'd hoped to convince her to tell him what it was, to let him help.

Every time he'd considered broaching the subject— telling her he worked in law enforcement and could help her with whatever had her so afraid—they'd ended up making love instead.

Not that Steve had minded that. The only time he didn't see shadows floating in Rosalyn's eyes was when they were filled with passion. He had hoped to convince her to stay the rest of the week with him and during that time get her to tell him what was really going on with her. To share whatever burdens she carried. And the secrets she was obviously keeping.

Starting with her last name.

But it soon became obvious Rosalyn wasn't out to grab coffee or go for a jog. Steve had known that from the beginning, although he hadn't wanted to face it. Someone who looked over her shoulder as much as Rosalyn, who'd been so willing to stay inside the bungalow even when there was a gorgeous beach right outside, wouldn't be going out for a casual walk.

Checking his wallet confirmed it. She'd taken every bit of his cash.

She'd played him.

Even now, six months later, the thought sat heavily in his gut. The time they'd spent together hadn't meant anything to Rosalyn. He was just a means to an end.

Steve had packed up his stuff that afternoon and returned to Colorado Springs. He'd been in a bad mood ever since. Obviously something everyone was aware of, from the conversation that had just occurred outside his door.

The thing was, he would've given Rosalyn the money—more if she'd needed it—if she had let him know what was going on. Would've done it without her having sex with him or waiting until he was asleep to steal it.

But she hadn't. She'd found him to be an easy mark and taken off.

Steve stood and walked over to the plastic evidence bag on his windowsill and picked it up. It held a glass inside. One from the bungalow that he knew contained Rosalyn's fingerprints.

Steve had brought it back with him like it was some damn souvenir or something.

"Hey, boss."

Steve put the bag back down quickly. "Brandon, hi."

"Liam is showing Cynthia pictures of the twins."

Steve rolled his eyes. "Who would've thought the great womanizer would become such a family man."

Brandon joined Steve at the window. "Just takes the right woman."

Brandon had found the right woman a couple of months ago—Omega behavioral analyst Andrea Gordon—and Steve couldn't argue the change it had brought about in the man. The peace it had brought both Brandon and Andrea.

"You brought that home from Florida, right?" Brandon asked, pointing to the evidence bag. "Prints, I'm assuming. But you've never run them."

Steve shrugged. Brandon was a certified genius and a profiler. Not much got past him.

"I'm assuming something happened with a woman down there. If I had to guess, I would say a one-night stand."

Sometimes Han was spooky good at his job. Steve shrugged again. "It was Florida. And you guys did pitch in to get me the romance package."

"Then I'm assuming she took off suddenly, probably while you were unaware."

"Why do you say that?" Steve crossed back over to his desk chair.

Brandon leaned a shoulder against the wall. "You

sure you want me to go into this? I didn't come here to profile you, Steve."

"No, please. Continue." Brandon was rarely wrong and Steve needed to hear what the man thought of his behavior.

"Okay, you met a woman. You were extremely interested in her. I would assume the relationship became intimate, but you didn't and still don't know much about her."

All right so far. Steve gestured for Brandon to continue.

"Something happened. Something not good. The fact that you have an evidence bag with a glass with her prints suggests that you want to know more about her. Who she is. But the fact that you haven't run them suggests that she hurt you personally in some way rather than actually committing a crime against you, in which case you would try to find and arrest her. She hurt your pride."

Actually, Rosalyn had done both, committed a crime and hurt his pride.

"And you're mad at yourself."

Steve's eyes narrowed. "Why do you say that?"

"You keep that bag in the center of the windowsill. You look out that window at least a dozen times a day. Every time you do, you're reminded of the woman who got the best of you. Who got past your guard, then hurt you. You want to remind yourself never to be weak like that again."

Steve leaned back in his chair. "I'm glad you're on our side, Han."

Brandon walked over to Steve's desk. "It's okay to

want to check on her, Steve. To see if she's okay. To be concerned about her even after she did whatever she did."

Now he was getting further off course. "You getting that from an evidence bag too?"

"No. I can tell that from knowing you for so many years. Nobody just gets the drop on you. You let this woman close to you for a reason—more than just a physical one. No matter how it all ended, you're still a little concerned about her."

A picture of Rosalyn's haunted blue eyes jumped into Steve's mind but he pushed it away. Rosalyn was a consummate actress. She'd faked passion with him, then stolen his money. She was lucky he wasn't running her prints—he was sure she'd end up in the system somewhere—and having her arrested.

He told himself it was because stealing less than $200 wasn't worth the taxpayers' money needed to have her arrested and put in jail for a few months.

It had nothing to do with being concerned for her.

"Well, most of your profile of me and this situation is correct, except for the last part. I don't have any concern about her." Steve smiled, but it was stiff, as if it had been so long the muscles seemed to have forgotten how. "Just want the reminder not to be a jackass again."

"Oh man, are we profiling Steve?" Liam asked from the doorway. "I missed all the good stuff."

Liam would probably make the worst profiler ever. The man didn't care how people thought, just wanted to understand the best way to bring down bad guys.

"Don't worry, Liam, I'll try to control myself and not use your own weapon against you."

Liam at least had the good grace to look sheepish. "Sorry about that, boss. I know I—"

"Don't worry about it." Steve cut him off. "I know I haven't been the easiest person to be around for the last few months."

"Are you kidding me? I have a wife trying to nurse newborn twins. She hasn't gotten a decent night's sleep since they were born. You are not the grumpiest person I know."

Steve snickered. "Glad to hear I at least beat out an exhausted new mother."

"Yeah, well, I keep my weapons away from her too." Liam grinned.

The two men took a seat. It was good to feel something besides anger. Listening to Brandon's profile had helped Steve realize it was time to let it all go.

Yeah, he'd been a fool and had gotten played. But now it was time to move on.

STEVE LEFT LATE that night and was back in the office early the next morning, as per his usual habits. Like always, Cynthia was in the office before Steve got there.

"Morning, Steve." She handed him a stack of papers as he came in. "I've got your overnight Washington, DC, briefings, your weekly Omega Division Directors' update and your Pensacola police briefings."

Steve took the papers from her. "Thanks."

As he got to the door to his office, he turned back. It was time. Past time.

"You can stop the Pensacola PD briefings. I don't need those anymore."

He didn't even know why he had started them in

the first place. Well, actually, he did. He figured Rosalyn would probably be arrested at some point. If she was a small-time crook preying on traveling salesmen, she would probably get arrested eventually.

What he really didn't know was what the hell he planned to do if her name came across his desk in an arrest report. Press charges himself? Or go get her released and keep her with him and make sure she never did anything that stupid again?

He shook his head, irritated with himself for his thoughts. He walked over to the evidence bag with the glass. He picked it up and carried it to the trash can by his desk. He hesitated just the briefest of moments before tossing it in.

It was time.

Steve set the division updates—the weekly reports that allowed all the directors to know what was happening in the different sectors of Omega—in one pile. He grabbed the Pensacola police reports and prepared to throw them in the trash.

A picture from that group caught his attention and brought him up short. A Jane Doe the Pensacola police hadn't been able to identify.

It was Rosalyn. She looked like she was sleeping peacefully.

But the picture was from the county morgue.

Rosalyn was dead.

Chapter Five

Steve caught the first flight he could get to Pensacola. Sadness and guilt weighed on him the entire time.

The prints on the glass in his office—immediately fished out of the trash—were being run right now. If Rosalyn was in any law enforcement system, Steve would have the full results by the time he met with the Pensacola police.

Damn it, he should have run them earlier. Should've gotten her information and gone after Rosalyn himself. Okay, maybe she might have had to do a short stint in prison for theft, but at least she would be alive.

Steve had known something was wrong, known Rosalyn was in serious trouble, but he hadn't been able to look past his wounded pride to see she got the help she needed.

And now it was too late.

He got the information about the prints via email as he was getting off the plane in Pensacola.

Rosalyn Mellinger.

Twenty-four years old from Mobile, Alabama.

Her prints actually weren't in any of the law enforcement databases; that's why the Pensacola PD hadn't been able to identify her. Cynthia had been able to identify Rosalyn from something to do with her juvenile record. She couldn't access the full record but had been able to link the print from the glass to the record.

Steve drove straight to the police department, which also housed the coroner's office. It was midafternoon but Steve was determined to identify Rosalyn's body today. Somehow he couldn't stand the thought of her sitting another night unidentified in the morgue.

The Pensacola county sheriff and the coroner were both waiting for Steve when he walked in.

"Agent Drackett." The sheriff, a portly man in his fifties, extended his hand for shaking. "Is agent the right title? I'm Sheriff Harvey Palmer."

"Just call me Steve." He shook the man's hand.

"This is Dwayne Prase, our county coroner." Steve shook his hand too.

They began walking down the hallway to the morgue.

"We really appreciate you coming all the way from Colorado," Sheriff Palmer said. "I have to be honest— I didn't expect your call."

"I don't know the victim in any official capacity. I met her when I was on vacation here six months ago. We spent a few days together. I recognized her immediately when the Jane Doe picture came across my desk."

"I see." The sheriff nodded and thankfully didn't ask why Steve would be getting police reports from Pensacola. "No one here has missed her at all. No missing-persons report or anyone asking about her. Her prints didn't show up in any of our computers."

Steve nodded. If he hadn't had access to the Omega

databases, he wouldn't have known anything about Rosalyn either.

"She was definitely murdered?"

Palmer nodded. "Yes, strangled. In her car in a parking lot."

"She'd been dead for hours before anyone found her," the coroner chimed in. "And has been here unidentified for nearly thirty-six hours."

Steve brought his fingers up to the bridge of his nose. There was so much he wished he'd done differently.

They reached the cold chamber of the morgue, where the body was being kept to reduce decomposition. Steve entered with the two men and saw the body was already on the table ready to be identified.

Prase pulled the sheet slowly off the body's face.

Steve hadn't realized how much he'd been praying there had been some type of mistake, that it wasn't really Rosalyn, but looking at her now, he couldn't deny it.

"That's her. That's Rosalyn Mellinger."

STEVE SPENT THE next couple of hours with Sheriff Palmer, filling out some paperwork. He'd asked the sheriff if his men would mind if Steve stuck around for a couple of days and helped in any way he could with the investigation. Thankfully, Palmer hadn't felt threatened by the offer and readily agreed.

He'd called back into Omega and let them know he'd be out for a few days. One thing about having a team as good as his: they could continue to function without him when necessary.

Steve planned to find Rosalyn's killer. It was the least he could do.

But not tonight. Tonight he was going to go back to the tiki bar where he'd met her and have a drink in her memory.

Steve decided to stay at the same hotel he'd used before. Not the romance package, but still a nice place. It was only a few blocks from the station. He checked in and unloaded his overnight bag. He took off his suit and changed into jeans and a T-shirt. No shorts and flip-flops this time.

He decided to walk to the tiki bar from his room even though it was through sand. He stopped for a minute as he reached the area where he and Rosalyn had sat and talked for so long that first night, partially because he wanted to take a moment to remember that place.

But also because Steve could feel eyes on him.

Someone was watching him.

As inconspicuously as he could manage, Steve turned. He didn't see anything to his left. He knelt down into the sand as if he'd found some great shell and spun to the right. No one there either.

Maybe this feeling was just a result of stress. God knew today had been stressful enough.

He stood back up and began walking to the bar.

It was a Wednesday now, not a Sunday like when he'd been here before. The TVs had some basketball games on, and the place wasn't nearly as full.

No Jimmy Buffett playing on the jukebox, no storm driving in beautiful women from outside.

Steve didn't plan to be here long so didn't get his

seat at the end of the bar. Instead just sat at the first seat he came to and ordered a beer.

He was only a few sips into it when he felt eyes on him again. Steve quietly paid the bartender in case he had to leave in a hurry but then sat back and eased himself casually around in the barstool.

No one seemed to be paying him much mind, but he'd been in law enforcement too long to ignore a gut feeling twice in one hour.

Somebody was following him. Probably had been since he left the police station.

Maybe it was the killer trying to see who had identified his victim. Or maybe hoping to make another victim out of Steve.

Steve felt adrenaline pump through him. Bring it on. There was nothing he'd like better than a physical altercation with Rosalyn's killer before arresting him. They would have to send the perp to the hospital before taking him to a holding cell.

Steve took a sip of his beer and allowed his vision to become slightly unfocused so he could better see everything happening in the room at once. After just a few moments he caught what he was looking for.

Someone out on the deck in a hooded jacket watching him through the window. The figure ducked as soon as Steve glanced his way.

Steve moved immediately but had to go out the side door to make it to the deck, losing valuable moments. The guy had already headed down the outer stairs and was moving quickly toward the closest set of hotels. Picking out his black jacket and hood was difficult in the darkening sky.

But Steve had no plan to let him get away.

Steve looked forward to the hotel buildings where the man obviously planned to go—his car was probably parked there. Then he ran down the back stairs, jumping down the last few. He began running up the path to the hotel also, but on a different path so the guy wouldn't look back and think Steve was following him and move faster.

Steve was going to come around the other side of the building and cut him off.

It was a risky plan, dependent on the perp not changing course, but Steve didn't dwell on it. He put all his effort into getting around the other side of the building before the person got there.

Racing through sand wasn't easy but Steve knew he was gaining ground. From the corner of his eye Steve could see the perp was slowing down. Probably because he didn't see Steve behind him. Or maybe he was trying to blend in with some other tourists now that he was closer to the hotel.

Steve didn't slow down as sand gave way to a sidewalk, then to the asphalt surrounding the hotel. Glancing over, he saw the hooded figure slip down a slim walkway between two buildings. This was his chance.

Steve forced another burst of speed out of his body. He had to make it around the corner and to the walkway before the guy got through and made it into the parking lot. Steve wouldn't have much chance of finding him then.

Steve barreled around the corner ready to make a flying tackle if necessary, but the guy wasn't there. He immediately scanned the parking lot but saw only one group of teenage girls getting into their car and two parents removing kids from car seats in another.

No hooded man. Damn it.

Steve squinted in the fading light. He could be hiding behind a vehicle. Or had made it around the corner and run the other way.

Something caught his attention away from the parking lot. About halfway down the corridor he'd been expecting the perp to run through, a head stuck out, looking the other way. It was the guy, looking for Steve but looking the wrong way.

Steve flattened himself against the wall and began making his way toward the man. He pulled out his weapon, although he kept it low and pointed to the ground. He didn't want to cause any panic for vacationers who might alert the suspect that Steve was coming up behind him.

Quickly but silently, Steve approached the hooded figure, who still watched the other way.

"I'm armed law enforcement," Steve said as he made his last few steps and pointed his Glock directly at the man. "Very slowly put your hands behind your head."

Steve saw the guy stiffen and stepped closer in case he tried to run again or fight. He was small, but Steve had seen plenty of small people who could do a lot of damage. Hell, he'd helped train some of the best himself.

Steve didn't have cuffs with him, so he'd have to call Sheriff Palmer to come make the arrest.

"Just stay right there," he said as he pulled his phone out of his pocket.

The guy began to turn around.

"Hey, did you hear me?" Steve poked him in the back with his weapon. "Just stay right where you are."

"Steve." The voice was soft. Almost a whisper, but it sent a bolt of electricity through him.

Steve did something he hadn't done in twenty years of law enforcement: lowered his weapon in shock.

This wasn't a man at all. It was a woman.

"Rosalyn?"

She reached up and lowered the hood of her Windbreaker as she turned completely around.

It was her. Beautiful black hair, gorgeous blue eyes. Even the splattering of freckles over her nose. Rosalyn was alive.

Which was impossible because he'd just ID'd her dead body a few hours ago. Steve didn't care. By whatever miracle she was here—and he would get her to explain it all, no doubt—he would take it.

He holstered his weapon and pulled her into his arms. Then yanked her back immediately, looking closer at the rest of her body.

Rosalyn was here. She was alive.

And unless he was very, very wrong, she was definitely pregnant.

Chapter Six

Steve stared down at her belly for a long time. He finally looked up at her face again.

There were so many questions in his eyes she hardly knew how to start answering them all.

His hand gently touched her stomach, so that's where she started.

"Yes, I'm pregnant. Six months."

It wasn't terribly difficult math, so she let him work out for himself that the baby was his. She didn't want to say it outright, because she wasn't sure if he would even believe her. They hadn't parted on the greatest of terms, after all.

He studied her for a long time without saying anything. Rosalyn just stood there. She was as surprised to see him as he was to see her.

"I just identified your dead body," he finally said.

Okay, maybe not *quite* as surprised.

"My twin sister," she whispered. "Lindsey Rose. I didn't know she was dead until today. I was coming into the police department when I saw you leaving."

She'd been skeptical about going to the police station anyway, knowing the Watcher would probably be waiting for her there. When she saw Steve exit the building, she'd been totally thrown.

What was he doing there?

Steve was the last person Rosalyn expected to see. His presence had to have something to do with Lindsey's death. Why else would he be here from Colorado?

"Have you been following me from the police station?"

"Yes."

Steve's eyes narrowed. "Why? To tell me about the baby? Why did you run when I saw you at the bar?"

He fired off the questions faster than she could answer them. Not that she knew how to answer them anyway.

She hadn't expected to see Steve. She'd been about to cross the street into the police station, knowing her sister was dead and the Watcher had found her again.

She was six months pregnant, alone, frightened and grieving. She'd pushed back the terror, so her only thought had been identifying her sister so Lindsey could have a proper burial.

Then Steve had walked out the door. He'd looked so strong. So capable of handling anything life threw at him.

Rosalyn had gotten in her car and followed him without even meaning to. When she saw he was going to the same hotel and then the same bar where they'd met, she'd felt a little hope inside.

Maybe he didn't hate her.

Maybe she could tell him about the baby.

Maybe she could tell him about the Watcher and everything that had happened.

She needed help.

But when his eyes had flown to her at the bar, obviously suspecting trouble, she'd panicked. She'd run— well, run as fast as her body would let her—to get away.

But she hadn't gotten away. He'd caught her and said—

He was law enforcement?

"You're a *cop*?"

He took a step closer, obviously trying to use his size to intimidate her. "You didn't answer my questions."

She couldn't get into the entire story now. They were too out in the open. "I will answer your questions, but not out here. You told me you were in management before."

Steve shrugged. "I never said what sort of management I was in. And I want answers to my questions before I arrest you."

"Arrest me for what?"

"How about the theft of nearly $200 six months ago?"

Rosalyn's face heated. "I'm sorry about that. I didn't have any other choice. I was desperate. My whole time with you I was pretty desperate."

That wasn't the right word, or at least she should've phrased it differently, she realized when he stiffened and stepped back. She hadn't meant that she'd spent time with him because she was desperate, but he'd obviously taken it that way.

"I guess your little souvenir from our time together—" he gestured at her belly "—wasn't what you wanted, then. Is the baby even mine?"

"Yes." She took a step toward him without even meaning to. "I know you probably don't believe me, but you're the only man I've been with for a long time." The only man she'd allowed herself to trust in a long time.

"Yeah, well, once the kid is born, there are paternity tests that are probably in our best interests to complete."

Rosalyn knew she shouldn't be hurt given what had happened between them but she couldn't help it. "Of course. I don't expect you to just believe me."

Now that the Watcher had found her again, she needed Steve's help whether he believed her or not. She had more than just herself to look out for. Steve didn't know the entire situation but at least she knew she could trust him.

Steve ran a hand through his hair. "Look, I'm not trying to be an ass. You've caught me off guard on multiple levels here. But I need some answers."

"Okay. I have a room at a hotel a few miles from here. Let's go there."

ROSALYN WAS ALIVE.

Rosalyn was alive *and* pregnant. Steve could hardly get his head around the first part, much less the second.

She was sitting right in front of him in a pretty scary run-down hotel room they'd driven to in her car, eating a packet of crackers. He was sitting in the desk chair that he'd pulled over and placed right in front of the bed just watching her. Like her eating crackers was the most interesting thing he'd ever seen.

Did she need more food than that? Was she taking care of herself? Had she been seeing a doctor throughout her pregnancy to make sure everything was okay?

Was the baby honestly his? They had used protection. But he knew accidents still happened.

He wanted to believe her when she'd said yes. She'd taken off her jacket and he could more clearly see the outline of her stomach under the T-shirt she wore. There was very definitely a baby bump. Not one that had her waddling or anything like that, but very definitely pregnant. Someone as petite as Rosalyn couldn't hide it.

He wanted to ask her all sorts of questions about her pregnancy but had so many other questions to ask that those got pushed to the back burner.

Steve sorted through important information for a living, made decisions on where Omega's Critical Response team would go and what they would do, based on his reading of a situation. Knowing what questions to ask to get the information he needed was his *job*. And lives depended on his ability to do it well.

But damned if he knew where to start with Rosalyn.

The dead body seemed the most reasonable place.

"So the woman I identified in the morgue—"

"Like I said, my identical twin, Lindsey Rose Mellinger. My mom—in a fit of soberness—thought it was quite clever."

Rosalyn and Lindsey Rose. "The reversal of each other. Well, almost."

She nodded. "Yeah. And it ended up being true in just about everything. We were twins, but we were complete opposites. Very different from each other except for how we looked."

"When was the last time you saw your sister alive?"

Tears came to Rosalyn's eyes, but she brushed them away. "At least a year and a half ago. We've never been close but grew even further apart as adults. Lindsey was in and out of drug rehab all the time. She still lived in Mobile."

"And that's where you're from?" Steve already knew the answer to that but wondered if she would lie.

"Yes, but I haven't lived there for nearly a year."

Steve wondered where she'd been for the past six months, but he'd get to that.

"Do you know anything about your sister's death?"

She shook her head. "No, but she was murdered, wasn't she?"

"What makes you say that?"

This time the tears overflowed before Rosalyn could wipe them away. "Lindsey was in Pensacola because I asked her to meet me. We were supposed to meet at a restaurant a few blocks from here two days ago, but she never showed up."

She gave him the name and address of a local café. Lindsey's body had been found inside her car very close to that area.

"Lindsey's pretty flighty," Rosalyn continued. "I thought she'd just gotten the day or time wrong. Or that she was high again. I didn't know she was dead until a waiter showed me a tiny section of the local paper that stated the police were looking for information about a deceased Jane Doe who looked exactly like me."

Rosalyn stood up and grabbed a tissue from the box

on the small desk. "I was coming by this afternoon to identify the body when I saw you."

"You said she did drugs a lot, so what makes you think she was murdered? Don't you think it's more likely something happened with her drug abuse?"

"Normally, yes." She sat back down. "But I suspect foul play because she was meeting me."

"I don't understand."

Rosalyn's blue eyes bore into him. "You saw her body, right?"

Steve nodded.

"I'll answer your questions, I promise. But first please tell me, was she murdered?"

Steve couldn't see any good in lying to her. "Yes, I'm sorry. She was strangled in her car."

Rosalyn began to cry quietly, holding her face in her hands. Steve moved to sit next to her. No matter what had happened between the two of them, he would never deny comfort to someone who had lost a family member.

"I had hoped you would tell me something different. That it was related to drugs," she finally said.

"I don't understand why you don't think it would've been." In Steve's experience, when regular people heard a family member had died, they did not assume it was murder. And if Lindsey had been involved in illegal drugs, Steve didn't know why Rosalyn didn't assume the murder wasn't centered around that.

Because Rosalyn knew something. Something she wasn't telling him.

"Rosalyn." He tilted a finger under her chin so she

was looking directly at him. "Tell me. Whatever is going on, I need you to tell me."

She tried to look away, but he wouldn't let her.

"I can't." Another tear slid silently down her cheek. "I can't risk you too."

Steve stared at the tiny woman—tiny, *pregnant* woman—determined to protect him. Why would she care about him if he was just someone she had scammed and robbed? Either way, he was getting to the bottom of all this.

"I can take care of myself, Rosalyn. Just tell me what's going on."

At first he didn't think she was going to answer, but finally she did.

"For the past year someone has been stalking me."

Steve sat up straighter. "Stalking you how?"

"Mostly he leaves notes. Ones he slides under my door while I'm sleeping at night." She shuddered. "Although on occasion he has emailed, texted or called me."

He'd been in law enforcement long enough to take stalkers very seriously. Especially ones who were close enough to leave notes under doors. That meant they were close and probably deadly. "What types of messages?"

"Never anything threatening. Not even 'We'll be together forever' stuff. Usually just little comments about something that has happened in my day."

Odd for a stalker, making it about her rather than about him. Stalkers were usually caught up in their own fantasy world and tried to make their victims a part of that.

"And you reported it?"

"Yes. I told my family first about a year ago. They just accused me of wanting attention. I decided to move across town, just to get rid of the weirdo, hoping that would stop it all."

"But it didn't?"

"The first night I moved into my new apartment, someone slid a note under my door."

Steve frowned. The guy had been following her closely. "Did you go to the local police?"

"Yes, I talked to them in Mobile, but I had thrown a lot of the letters away, so they didn't believe it was anyone wishing to do me harm."

It was easy to be frustrated with the Mobile police for doing nothing to help Rosalyn, but the truth was, funds were always limited in local departments. If the notes weren't threatening Rosalyn in any way, it would be easy to not give them or her much attention.

She stood up and began walking back and forth.

"It got so bad that after about a month I chose to just leave town. I had a pretty big savings account, so I quit my job and decided to go somewhere different. Anywhere different. I didn't have a moving truck, didn't grab a bunch of suitcases—I just got in my car one morning and left."

She stopped walking for a minute.

"I ended up in Dallas. Thought it would be a cool town to vacation in while I was losing my annoying little follower. Thought I had done it too, until the second night. Another note under my door mentioning the crème brûlée I had eaten at dinner."

She wasn't looking at him, but he could hear the fear in her voice.

"I left just minutes later. Drove all around to make sure no one was following me. Ended up in Shreveport. I went straight to the police station."

It wasn't the best of plans, since nothing had happened in their jurisdiction, but Steve didn't tell Rosalyn that. She would've been better off going to the Dallas police.

But a note that mentioned a dessert probably wouldn't have been taken seriously there either.

"Nobody wanted to listen to me, but this one detective, Johnson, offered to meet me after he got off his shift. I told him everything, and he helped me. Or he tried."

"What did he do?"

She began rubbing her hands on her legs, a nervous gesture he didn't think she was aware of.

"I showed him what notes I had kept. He told me to keep them all, and any I got from now on, in a box. And he gave me a notebook and showed me how to keep track of everything that the Watcher did."

He reached over and grabbed her hands so she would stop the rubbing. "The Watcher?"

"Yeah, that's what I call him. I've kept everything since Detective Johnson showed me what to do."

"And did he do anything with it? Did it go any further?"

"Unfortunately, he died of a heart attack the next day."

Steve's head snapped up. "Was he old?"

"Maybe fifty. And in pretty good shape."

"That's a damn unfortunate coincidence." And probably a devastating blow for Rosalyn, to have found someone who wanted to help, then died.

"I thought so too until I got an anonymous email the next day about a drug that caused heart attacks."

"What?"

"The Watcher killed Detective Johnson. He's killed everyone I've told about him. I'm afraid you'll be next."

Chapter Seven

Steve didn't believe her.

He wasn't overt in his disbelief, didn't mock her or anything like that. But she could tell he didn't think the Watcher was actually a credible threat. He thought Detective Johnson, a fifty-year-old policeman, had died of a heart attack.

It certainly happened all the time. Police work was stressful.

Her sister was also dead, but she'd been a drug addict. That happened all the time too.

She didn't tell him about Shawn, the mechanic, who'd also died after she'd told him about the Watcher. Because she could already tell Steve thought she was exaggerating.

She'd recognized the placating look. The attempt to figure out how to convince her of reason without offending her. He didn't want to add to her stress, but he also didn't think there was anything sinister to her story.

Not to mention he was still pretty shocked about her reappearance and pregnancy. So she should probably cut him a little slack.

She hadn't planned to drag him into this. Because whether he wanted to believe her or not, she knew it was true: the Watcher would try to kill him next.

Rosalyn wanted to run, to try to keep Steve safe. But she couldn't anymore. She had to face the fact that soon it wouldn't just be her. She'd have the baby. She couldn't go back on the run with a child in tow.

She'd had six months of relative peace. Although she'd lived in fear every single night of the Watcher contacting her, he hadn't. Rosalyn didn't know why. She'd thought he'd given up, decided to leave her alone.

She'd made a huge error, she realized now, contacting her sister. It had not only cost Lindsey her life, but put Rosalyn back on the Watcher's radar.

She knew she wouldn't escape him again. Not without help.

Steve turned to her. "Look, let's just sleep on everything tonight. We can discuss this more in the morning."

She nodded. Maybe if she showed him the notes, he'd take her more seriously. Plus, she knew the questioning was nowhere near done on either side.

He was a cop and had deliberately withheld that information from her. She wasn't mad, but it changed some things. Maybe he could help protect her from the Watcher.

Of course, Detective Johnson had been in law enforcement too, and the Watcher had killed him. But that had been before she had realized how far the Watcher would go. Until Johnson's death Rosalyn had assumed only she would be his victim. She knew better now.

When they met tomorrow, she would have to make sure Steve understood the danger he was in.

"Okay, what time do you want to meet tomorrow?"

Steve looked at her like she'd lost her mind. "I'm not leaving you here. You're coming with me."

She hadn't been expecting that. "Why?"

"Multiple reasons. One, I don't trust that you're not going to be gone again in the morning."

Rosalyn felt her face heat but didn't say anything.

"Two, by your very own account you have a stalker and possibly a murderer after you. I'm not sure what all the facts are in this case, but I intend to find out. You can believe I won't be leaving you alone as I do it, especially not if you're carrying my child."

Rosalyn felt relief wash through her. Steve might not believe her completely but at least he was willing to look into it. And help protect her and the baby.

"Now, I will stay in this fleabag motel if you really insist on remaining here. But I would prefer we go to my hotel." He glanced around in distaste, then looked straight at her. "Either way, you can plan on spending tonight—every night until we figure out this stalker situation and the baby is born—with me."

He obviously didn't necessarily believe the baby was his, but at least he was willing to try to keep Rosalyn safe until he knew for sure. She wasn't sure whether to be thankful or offended.

But to stay here when he had a nicer place would just be foolish.

"Okay. Just let me get my stuff."

He took her duffel bag and walked her to her car. He took the key from her and put her bag in the trunk.

"Have you been going from town to town for the last six months?"

Rosalyn bit her lip. Telling him the truth, that the Watcher hadn't contacted her since she'd last been in Pensacola, wasn't going to help him believe her about how dangerous her stalker was.

She didn't know why the Watcher hadn't contacted her while she'd been hidden at the Ammonses' home in Georgia, had lived in constant fear that he would, but she'd been thankful for the reprieve.

"Let me go pay for the room. You stay here," he said.

"No, I'll pay. I can afford it."

One of his eyebrows raised. "I don't even want to know how you got the money."

"I didn't steal it, all right? That was a one-time thing and only because I was desperate."

He still didn't look like he believed it.

"You stay here with the car and I'll go pay." She gave him the evilest glare she could.

Which only made him smile. "Fine, you pay. I'll be here."

The motel office was at the other end of the parking lot, close to the main street. Rosalyn was aware she was marching off in a huff and had neither the size nor stature to pull that off with any authority, especially when she looked like she'd swallowed half a basketball. She knew Steve was probably laughing at her, but she didn't care.

At least if he was laughing at her, he wasn't threatening to arrest her. Not that she really thought he planned to.

She went inside and paid her bill, a little mad that

they still charged her for two nights even though she'd stayed only one. Regardless, she wasn't going to let Steve pay. At least the extra cost didn't cause her the panic it once would have, since she now had some money saved up from being able to work the last six months. She signed the paperwork, paid her bill and walked back out the door toward her car.

"I'll pay you back all that money, you know," she called out, moving directly toward him.

He walked toward her. "It's not necessary to pay me back. You can—"

Rosalyn heard the roar of an engine and turned. A car, headlights off, was screeching toward her, swerving back and forth.

"Hey, look out!" someone yelled from a second-floor walkway.

Rosalyn couldn't figure out which way to move to get out of the car's oncoming path. All she knew was that it was going to hit her.

She was still frozen in place, certain of her own demise, when a huge force hit her from the side.

Steve.

He pulled her to his chest and continued their momentum out of the car's direct path, somehow managing to spin them so he took the weight of the fall.

Both of them covered her belly with their arms.

They were on the ground for only a split second before Steve jumped back up to his feet. He pulled his gun from the holster and pointed it at the car.

But the driver put the car in Reverse and began speeding at Steve. The vehicle hit him and knocked him backward.

"Steve!" Rosalyn screamed from where she lay on the ground.

He sat up and got one shot off, but when the car sped toward him again, he had to stop and roll to the side out of the way. He began firing again.

Rosalyn scooted herself back, unsure what the car would do. But thankfully, it sped off.

Steve ran over to her and placed his hands over hers on her stomach. "Are you okay? I'm sorry I hit you so hard."

Her heart was still racing but she didn't think she was injured. "Better you than the car. I'm fine. And I'm pretty sure the baby is okay. You took the brunt of the fall."

The manager ran out of the office. "Oh my gosh, are you guys all right? I just called 911. That guy had to have been drunk."

Two other people ran out from the building. "We saw the whole thing. Did anybody get the license plate?"

They all began to talk over each other.

Rosalyn tuned them out and started to stand up, but Steve's hands kept her gently on the ground. "Just stay there, okay? There's an ambulance coming. Let's just be safe and wait."

She nodded. Her heart still beat erratically but otherwise she didn't feel too bad. But Steve was right—better to let them check her out, just in case.

"Damn drunk driver. You guys are lucky to be alive," the manager said. "I mean, the way he reversed like that? Couldn't figure out which way was forward."

Rosalyn looked over at Steve. His eyes said the same thing as hers. That had been no drunk driver.

"Are you okay?" she asked him. "You're the one who got hit by the car."

He let out a small groan as he sat down on the asphalt beside her. "Yeah, nothing broken, I'm pretty sure."

Activity buzzed around them, but Rosalyn and Steve just sat in silence. His hand was never far from her stomach. Soon the ambulance and police showed up. Rosalyn was assisted onto the stretcher and put inside the ambulance while Steve talked to the cops.

She didn't know exactly what he said to them, but within minutes the ambulance was on its way and Steve was riding beside her. He left her side only when they arrived at the hospital, to talk to some member of the staff.

Again, Rosalyn couldn't hear but twenty minutes later she was being seen by the hospital's chief OB-GYN physician even though it was nearly ten o'clock at night. Dr. Puglisi had her hooked up to an ultrasound machine as soon as she heard what happened.

"There," Dr. Puglisi said, pointing to the monitor. "Good, strong heartbeat. Baby is absolutely fine."

Tears poured down Rosalyn's cheeks as she grabbed Steve's hand beside her. "Thank God."

"A woman's body is pretty amazing at protecting the fetus growing inside it. It generally takes more than a fall to cause real problems." Dr. Puglisi moved the ultrasound wand. "Do you know the gender of the baby?"

Rosalyn shook her head. "Not yet. It was scheduled for my next appointment."

"Would you like to know?"

Rosalyn looked over at Steve but he just shrugged. "That's completely up to you."

She tried not to show the hurt she felt by his nonchalance but knew she couldn't blame Steve. It was too soon.

Rosalyn turned back to the doctor. "Yes, I'd like to know, if you can tell."

The doctor smiled. "Congratulations—your strong resilient baby is a boy."

Chapter Eight

He was going to have a son.

Dr. Puglisi had run a number of tests on Rosalyn, just to double-check that everything was okay. That she was healthy, the baby was healthy and nothing was going to creep up on them unawares.

Some of the tests she did were to establish the gestational age of the child.

Every indication was that the fetus was twenty-five weeks developed. That would mean he was conceived six months ago.

Steve knew that didn't mean the baby was his. But it was definitely a step closer.

The most important thing right now was that both Rosalyn and the baby were healthy. His flying tackle hadn't hurt either of them in any way.

When he'd seen that car speeding toward Rosalyn his heart had stopped. Only years of training, his body responding almost before his mind did, had him moving forward to get her out of the way.

Drunk driver, his ass.

Steve might possibly have believed it if the guy hadn't backed up to run over him.

Someone had been trying to kill Rosalyn or Steve or both of them. He'd made it look like he was a drunk driver, but after everything Rosalyn had told him, that was one coincidence too many.

Funny thing was, until the attack happened, he hadn't really believed Rosalyn about her Watcher theory. To Steve, her description of the situation broke too many of the typical patterns that would be found in a stalker committed enough to kill people.

He'd spent the last hour in a room the hospital had lent him for privacy, on the phone with Sheriff Harvey Palmer. He explained about Rosalyn and her twin, Lindsey. Explained how Lindsey's prints weren't in the system but Rosalyn's were, although he still didn't know why.

Steve also told Palmer what had happened with the car. A dark two-door Toyota with no plates wasn't going to be particularly helpful, but the sheriff agreed to run the description against other incidents in the area. Maybe they'd get lucky.

Steve finished the call by telling Palmer he'd be taking Rosalyn with him out of Florida.

He was going to take her to Colorado Springs. Back to Omega Critical Response headquarters. If they were fighting some villain intent on hurting Rosalyn and her baby, Steve planned to fight on his own turf.

Once he finished with Sheriff Palmer, he called his office.

"Steve Drackett's office."

"Angela, it's me." Someone was in Steve's office twenty-four hours a day, seven days a week to be able to field calls that might come from as far up as the White House. Angela tended to work the evening shifts.

"Hey, boss. I thought you were taking a couple of personal days."

"I was, but my situation has changed. I'm going to need you to book me two tickets on a flight from Pensacola to Colorado Springs for as early as possible tomorrow. Me and a Rosalyn Mellinger."

"Okay, no problem. I'll text you with the details."

"Anything exciting happening around the office?"

"All in all, a pretty quiet day. If you can believe it."

A *quiet day* might have only meant there were no events threatening national security.

"I'm glad to hear it. I'll be back tomorrow."

"See you then, sir."

A doctor had already looked over Steve's wounds— some road rash and bruises—and declared him free to go. What had happened tonight could've been much worse.

He walked down the hallway and saw Rosalyn joking with one of the nurses. He was struck again by her natural beauty and animation.

It could've been much, much worse.

He'd spent six months angry with her, followed by a day of terrible sadness when he thought she was dead. He'd then been given the precious gift of a second chance when he'd found out she was alive.

Her smile still took his breath away just like it had six months ago.

"You ready to go?" he asked her.

She jumped down from the table. "Yep. Dr. Puglisi said I was done as soon as you were."

"Good. It's getting pretty late. I think we both could use some sleep. We'll go back to my hotel like we'd originally planned."

A uniformed officer had driven Rosalyn's car over from the scene of the accident at Steve's request. He opened the door for her to get in and made his way over to the driver's side.

He eased slowly out of the parking lot and began to drive. He didn't go directly to the hotel, instead took leisurely routes going nowhere near where they would be staying.

After an hour Steve was absolutely positive no one was following them. He'd actually been sure of it for twenty minutes before that, but Rosalyn had fallen asleep and waking her up seemed heartless. She'd had a hell of a day. First Steve pulling a gun on her, then someone trying to kill her. Not to mention dealing with her sister's recent death.

She deserved a nap.

They had so much they needed to talk about. He needed to find out all the details she had about the Watcher. Needed to know where she'd been for the last six months.

Needed to tell her that he was the director of an elite law enforcement agency and was probably more uniquely situated to protect her than anyone else. Even though he'd almost been killed today.

Yes, it was possible it was a drunk driver who had nearly run them over, but Steve would still be on high guard until he knew exactly what it was they were up against.

He drove around a few more minutes before pulling the car up to his hotel on the beach. He got out and looked around for a few minutes, making sure no one had picked them up in the last few minutes. Unlikely but possible.

Nothing. It was completely quiet in the parking lot. The beach was deserted also. All to be expected at nearly midnight on a Wednesday.

Steve walked over and got Rosalyn's duffel bag out of the trunk. She was still clutching her tote bag in her arms, just like she had been when he'd known her six months ago.

He opened her door and nudged her gently on the shoulder. "Hey, Sleeping Beauty, let's get you inside so you can sleep properly."

Her eyes barely opened but she got out of the car. He put an arm around her and led her through the lobby and up the elevator to their room on the seventh floor. He used his key card to get in.

This room was definitely less romantic than the setup six months ago. But from the look in Rosalyn's tired eyes, she didn't care about romance tonight.

"I'm just going to go straight to bed. Is that okay?" She lay down on the bed, on top of the covers, shoes still on. Evidently, having only one bed didn't bother her. She was sound asleep again.

Steve set her duffel bag on the chair and walked over to her. He untied and slipped off her athletic shoes. He then lifted her body with one arm—it shouldn't be that easy; if they hadn't just been reassured by one of the best doctors in the area that Rosalyn was perfectly healthy, Steve would've worried much more about how little she weighed—so he could tuck her under the blankets.

She never even stirred.

Steve shook his head, smiling. She was like a child. He didn't know if that was how she normally slept or if it was a product of exhaustion, pregnancy and stress.

It had been a long day. Steve took a shower, wincing at the sting of the water against his scrapes, and changed into fresh clothes.

Tomorrow he would have Rosalyn in Colorado. He realized she hadn't actually agreed to that yet. He wasn't trying to keep the information a secret, but neither was it up for negotiation. Steve needed to figure out what was going on. The Critical Response Division headquarters was the best place for him to do that.

The body of Rosalyn's sister still needed to be taken care of, but Rosalyn's mother would have to do that. He hoped Rosalyn wouldn't fight him about going to Colorado.

Not because he wouldn't take her if she did. He would still take her. It would just make it much more difficult.

But he'd fight that battle if he came to it. Right now she was sleeping peacefully and he should do the same.

He slid next to her into the king-size bed. His body wanted to grab her and pull her into his arms, but he knew that wasn't wise. Too many unresolved issues between them. Until he knew exactly what was happening, how much he could trust her, he knew he needed to keep his distance.

He looked over at Rosalyn, who had turned onto her

side in an attempt to get more comfortable. She looked innocent, lovely, fragile.

But in his line of work he'd learned how very easy it was for looks to deceive.

He would keep on his side of the bed. It was better for everyone that way.

STEVE WOKE UP and immediately sensed something was wrong.

Rosalyn lay completely snuggled in his arms, draped over him like a blanket. So much for keeping his distance from her.

But that wasn't what was wrong.

He looked over at the window. No light was peeking through, so it was obviously still night. He estimated about four o'clock in the morning.

What had awakened him?

He listened for any sounds that would be foreign. Someone trying to break into the room or yells from farther away.

Nothing.

Then he smelled it. Smoke. Too heavy to be just some cigarette somebody was toking on illegally on a balcony.

He shook Rosalyn. "Wake up, sweetheart."

She just mumbled and tried to move away from the hands disturbing her sleep. Steve shook her again. "Rosalyn, come on, you need to wake up." He pulled her until she was in a sitting position.

"What's going on?" she asked, blinking multiple times. "Is it morning?"

"There's trouble, I'm pretty sure."

He ran over to the door. He could see smoke seeping under the crack. He ran back and grabbed the hotel phone. As soon as someone answered, he barked out, "I'm in room 742. There's a fire in the hallway but the alarm isn't sounding. You need to call the fire department and get some sort of alarm working."

He didn't wait for the person to answer. He grabbed one of Rosalyn's shoes. "Can you put these on or do you need help?"

"I can do it. I'm slow, but I can get them."

He handed her one shoe and put the other on her foot himself. "We're going to have to get out of here. I'm not sure how bad the smoke and fire will be."

She grabbed her tote bag and pulled it over her shoulder. Fine, she could take that, but the rest of the stuff would have to stay.

He stood and led her to the bathroom. "Soak these towels. We'll keep them over our faces to protect us from the fire and smoke as best we can."

She began running water over them as he went to check the door again. The smoke was even heavier under the crack.

He opened the door slightly to see exactly what they were up against. He couldn't see three feet down the hall, the smoke was so thick. There was no way they'd be able to wait for the fire department to get up to their floor.

He shut the door, taking the wet towels from her. "It's bad out there. We're not going to be able to see much of anything. But we need to make it to the stairs."

"I don't know where they are." Panic pinched her face. "Are they near the elevator?"

"No." As a force of habit Steve had memorized the general layout of the hotel when he'd checked in. "They're a little bit farther. Just keep hold of my hand, no matter what."

She nodded, eyes big. He wrapped one of the wet towels around the lower part of her face. "I'm not sure the extent of the fire, but the smoke is thick out there. It's going to be rough. Stay low and breathe through the towel as much as possible."

When he opened the door again, he immediately felt heat to the right. The fire was closer than it had been moments ago.

And blocking their way to the stairs.

"We're going to have to go to the far staircase," he told Rosalyn. "Stay with me no matter what."

She nodded and he pulled the door open farther. Smoke immediately filled their room. Steve bent at the waist to get lower than the worst of the smoke in the hall. He knew bending that way would be difficult for Rosalyn. He was glad she was significantly shorter than he was to start with.

He lost all visibility only a few feet from their hotel room. He had to rely on his instincts and his mind's ability to process spatial data to get them to where they needed to be.

He could feel Rosalyn's small hand in his and knew that if he made a mistake, missed the door to the stairs or turned down the wrong hall, it could mean their deaths.

About halfway to where he estimated the stairs were, the smoke got so thick they had to crawl. Steve's eyes burned, although the wet towel at least protected his throat from the worst of the smoke.

He turned back to Rosalyn. Tears were streaming from her eyes. He knew his looked the same.

"Pull the towel all the way over your face," he yelled back at her. "I'll guide you out."

She didn't argue, just pulled the towel past her nose, over her eyes. It wouldn't help her for long, but it had to be better than nothing.

She was putting her trust in him completely to guide her out. He wouldn't let her down.

He crawled as rapidly as he could—feeling her hand on his ankle as she crawled behind him—until he found what he hoped was the right door. If not, they would be in dire straits. He could feel heat licking behind them.

The sound of glass breaking came from the other end of the hall, probably firefighters, but they wouldn't get the blaze and smoke under control quickly enough to help Rosalyn and Steve.

Steve reached up from his crawl to the door handle and sighed in relief when it opened.

They were at the stairs. Steve dragged Rosalyn inside the much cooler stairwell. People were running down the stairs, some crying, some screaming.

Steve stood and scooped Rosalyn up in his arms. He pulled the towel down from her face to find her looking out at him with those blue eyes.

"I'm okay," she whispered, voice a little husky. "I can walk."

He shook his head. He wasn't going to take a chance on her getting trampled or knocked down the stairs by someone in a panic.

He'd almost lost her twice today. And that was *after* he'd already ID'd her dead body.

He carried her to safety himself.

Chapter Nine

Rosalyn found herself being checked out by Dr. Puglisi for the second time in eight hours. Another ultrasound.

And thank God again both she and the baby were all right.

"I can admit you if you want, especially since it seems like fate wants you here in the hospital." Dr. Puglisi peered over her medical chart at Rosalyn. "But honestly, there's no reason for you to stay."

Rosalyn's eyes and throat hurt, like Steve had told her his did. Neither of them had inhaled enough smoke to do any real damage, thanks to Steve's quick thinking and ability to get them to the stairwell and out of the smoke rapidly.

"You're fortunate, of course," the doctor continued. "Both times tonight. Especially for someone who seems to be a magnet for trouble."

"I don't want to stay at the hospital if I don't have to, and if the baby is safe." Rosalyn put a hand protectively over her stomach.

"That little guy is perfectly fine. As a matter of fact, any day now you're going to be feeling him move more pronouncedly."

"All I've felt is like I have bubbles in my stomach all the time."

Dr. Puglisi smiled at her. "Those bubbles, the fluttery feeling, is your son."

"It is?" Rosalyn looked over at Steve. He was looking as shocked as she felt.

"Trust me." The doctor smiled again, then turned toward the door. "It won't be long until it's less like bubbles and more like karate kicks. Now, please, don't let me see you back here again tonight."

The doctor left and Rosalyn turned to Steve. He'd been by her side on the ride to the hospital—he'd driven them himself this time instead of taking an ambulance—and the entire time she'd waited to see Dr. Puglisi. He'd been pretty quiet that whole time too, pensive. The only time he really talked had been when he'd stepped out into the hallway to discuss something with someone from the sheriff's office. He'd also been back and forth on his phone all night.

"I'm going to take a shower." She slid her legs over the side of the hospital bed. They'd been given a private room with a bathroom; she might as well make use of it. She had a change of clothes in her tote bag.

"Good idea. I'll take one as soon as you're done." He walked beside her to the door, as if he was afraid she might need help.

"I'm okay," she told him. "I didn't get hurt."

He flattened his lips, narrowed his eyes, obviously upset. They'd both almost been killed twice tonight, so his anger was justified.

She wanted to talk to him about the fire. That had to have been just a terrible coincidence, right?

Or had the Watcher been so close he'd followed them or heard them talking about where they would be staying.

Rosalyn couldn't stop the shudder that ripped through her at the thought.

Steve was close enough to see it. "Sure you're okay?"

No, she wasn't sure she was okay. The opposite. And now she had dragged Steve down the rabbit hole with her.

A dark, dangerous rabbit hole where someone was determined to kill everyone who got close to her. And now it looked like maybe the Watcher was trying to kill her too.

She opened her mouth to ask Steve what he thought, what they should do. But he put a finger over her lips before she could get the words out.

"Shower. You'll feel better. You're safe here—we both are. Let's take advantage of that."

Rosalyn nodded. He was right.

"Do you mind if I borrow your cell phone while you're in there?"

"I don't have one. It was one of the first things I got rid of."

"You haven't had one since you've come back to Pensacola?"

She shook her head. "I haven't had one since the Watcher followed me to Dallas and sent me a series of texts. I destroyed it. Thought it might be the way he was following me."

"Smart girl. I was thinking the same thing."

She shrugged. "I didn't want to give him any extra means of being able to communicate with me."

"Okay."

Steve was right—the shower did help her feel better. Or at least washed away the smell of the smoke that had almost taken their lives.

Steve took one after her but didn't have a set of his own clothes to change into. A nurse brought a set of scrubs for him to wear, as well as a T-shirt.

Steve made a hot doctor as well as law enforcement officer.

Which was another thing they needed to talk about. Exactly what he did in law enforcement. Just add that to the list of all the stuff they still needed to talk about.

Less than an hour after changing they walked out of the hospital. Steve hadn't said much to her during that time, but he definitely had a plan.

"Do you want to tell me what exactly the plan is?" she asked as they got back into her car.

"I'm a cop who works in Miami. I've booked us a flight there that leaves in a couple of hours."

Of all the things he might have said, that wasn't what she'd expected. "You told me you were from Colorado."

He looked over at her, eyes narrowed. "I guess neither of us was telling the truth that night."

Rosalyn knew she had stolen from him. She was the one who had left him without a word. But somehow finding out that he had been lying about things he'd told her during their time together hurt her. He'd obviously wanted to make sure she could never track him down.

He winced. "Rosalyn—"

She sat up straighter in the seat. "No, you're right. We were both dishonest. And you don't have to take me with you now. As a matter of fact, that's probably better."

"No, you'll stay with me."

Why did he need her to stay with him now when he had gone out of his way to make sure she wouldn't be able to find him six months ago? She wanted to argue further but he had pulled into the parking lot of a superstore.

"Let's go. I need some clothes and you'll need some other stuff."

"Can't this wait until we get to Miami?" Why would he want to buy clothes here when he'd be back to his own home and stuff in just a couple of hours? His scrubs were unusual, but not overly so.

"No. Let's go." He got out of the car and went around to her side. "Bring your bag, everything."

She left the sweater in the seat and got out.

"No, bring that too."

"But I'm not cold."

He grabbed it out of the seat. "Bring it all anyway. Let's go."

She barely resisted rolling her eyes at his gruff tone. What had happened to the man who had been talking to her so kindly—trying to understand everything about what had been happening to her over the past year—a few hours ago at her run-down hotel room?

This gruff stranger had replaced him. He didn't seem to want to talk to her at all.

Maybe it was the two near-death experiences in one night since hanging around her. She couldn't blame him for that. Whether he was in law enforcement or not, it looked like Rosalyn might be back on her own again soon.

His actions inside the store didn't reassure her. He grabbed a cart, then kept her right next to him as they went through both the women's section, where he told her to grab jeans and a shirt, and men's, where they did the same for him.

He even grabbed underwear for both of them. When she tried to protest that she'd had a spare set in the tote bag, he ignored her and grabbed a set anyway. He pulled her to the dressing room, which was thankfully empty of everyone, including an attendant, since it was nearly six o'clock in the morning.

"Change all your clothes." He turned and walked toward the men's changing room.

Rosalyn had had just about enough of the man-handling.

"Look, I don't know exactly what your problem is, although honestly, I can understand if you're upset because of both the drunk-driver guy and the fire. But let's just talk about it, okay?"

Steve looked at her for a long time, then finally just turned away again. "No, not right now."

She could actually feel her eyes bugging out of her head. "Not right now? What is the matter with you?"

"Just go put on the other clothes."

"Maybe I'm just fine in the clothes I'm in. Have you thought of—"

The air rushed out of her body as he grabbed her by the arms and walked forward—forcing her backward into the dressing room. He went in right along with her and didn't stop until her back was up against the wall and he was pressed all the way up against her.

She would've thought he'd lost his mind if she hadn't been so turned on by the feel of him pressed against her. His mouth was just inches from hers and she couldn't stop staring at it.

But his lips didn't kiss her. Instead he dipped his head right next to her ear.

"You're bugged."

At first all she felt was the delicious heat from his breath on her earlobe. Then his whispered words made their way through her desire-addled brain.

"What—?"

She barely got the words out before his lips were on hers. She realized it was a kiss to stop her from saying anything that would give away the information about the bug, but she still couldn't stop her arms from circling up around his shoulders.

His lips moved back down her jaw until he was at her ear again.

"It's important that we not say anything that gives away that we know. I'll explain more later, but right now, we need to ditch everything."

Rosalyn nodded.

"Ahem, excuse me, mister. Men aren't allowed in the ladies' dressing room." A young store associate peeked his head into the room. "I'm afraid you'll have to change in the men's section."

Steve nodded and looked at Rosalyn on the way out. "Everything. Okay?"

As soon as Steve and the clerk left, Rosalyn closed the door and stripped off all her clothes.

A bug? Like a transmitting device?

She'd thought maybe her car was being tracked but hadn't considered some sort of tracking device on her clothing. But as she thought of it more, she cursed herself for being so obtuse. All those times she had thought the Watcher was in her head, he'd really just been on her clothes.

That even explained why sometimes he waited many days between contacting her but sometimes he communicated with her more than once within a few hours.

Because some clothes were bugged and some weren't.

Most of her clothes had been destroyed last night in the fire, along with her duffel bag. She tore off the rest and put on the new clothes Steve had left her. Everything changed, down to a new pair of socks and athletic shoes, bile caught in her throat the whole time.

She was just coming out of the changing room as an alarm started blaring overhead. Steve was standing, waiting for her. He turned to the clerk.

"What does that alarm mean? Fire?"

The kid shook his head. "No. I don't think so. I haven't worked here very long but I don't remember that one from my training. Tornado, maybe?"

Steve grabbed her hand. "We've got to go."

"I'm ready. All new clothes."

"Your bag has to go too. It could also easily be tracked."

She hated to give up the bag—it had been a part of

every single move she'd made for nearly a year—but didn't argue. Steve had another similar one he'd grabbed.

"I want to keep my notebook—is that okay? It has all entries about the Watcher."

Steve took it and flipped through it. "It looks clean."

She also took out her money and driver's license. Everything else—makeup, pens, knickknacks—got thrown in the trash with the pen.

The siren suddenly cut off. "It must have been a drill," the clerk muttered.

Steve looked at the guy's name tag. "Hey, Paul, you want to make a hundred dollars?"

Paul stood up. "Am I going to get fired for it?"

"No. I just need you to take the tags off all these clothes and pay for them up at a register. Any change left over is yours to keep."

Nobody had to ask Paul twice. He took the money and the tags from their clothes and left.

Steve took Rosalyn's hand and they walked toward the front.

"Should we do something with our old clothes?"

Steve shook his head. "I found two transmitting devices in your clothes. There's no telling how many more there might be. Hopefully, leaving them in the dressing room will throw your stalker off."

"And we're just going to waltz out the front door?"

"Yep."

"Isn't that dangerous?"

"I think the siren was an attempt to get us to do something stupid like run out the back door. Instead we'll just walk out the front like everyone else."

"And get on a flight to Miami."

"Nope. We were never going to Miami. I was just hoping to mislead whoever might be listening to our conversation."

"Oh. So you really are from Colorado?"

"Yep. And that's where we're headed. That's the best place for me to keep you safe."

Chapter Ten

"We're driving to Colorado Springs? Won't that take like three days?"

They were on their way, via rental car, and were already out of Florida.

"A day and a half at most. Barely more than it would have taken to fly, given the stopovers."

When Steve's assistant had sent him the flight list, they'd all looked pretty miserable: late starts, long layovers. When he'd found the transmitting device on Rosalyn's sweater, he'd known he had to get her out of there right away. Waiting ten hours for a flight wasn't an option.

He glanced over at her. "It's the best way, I promise. It got us out of Florida the quickest. Hopefully your stalker thinks we're on our way to Miami."

"That's how he's known where I was." Rosalyn shook her head. "I thought he might have some sort of tracker in my car, so I ditched it a couple of times. But he always found me."

"I don't know how you've kept away from him for the past few months." The thought of Rosalyn—alone and pregnant—trying to stay ahead of a killer sent ice through Steve's veins. It was all he could do to stop from grabbing her hand, which sat in her lap.

Hell, it was all he could do not to pull over the car at the first hotel and make love to her for a few days. Away from all the crazy surrounding her life and the fanatic trying to hurt her.

"Actually, I haven't heard from him since I last saw you in Pensacola. He left a note under your hotel room door and that's why I left."

He looked at her. *"What?"*

She shrugged. "For six months I haven't heard anything from the Watcher."

Steve brought his eyes back to the road. "No, go back. The Watcher left you a note at my hotel six months ago?"

"He slid it under the door that second night."

"Do you remember what it said?" Now Steve could appreciate why she wanted to keep the notes so badly.

"No, I try not to remember, because it would drive me a little crazy. That's why I write them down in my notebook." Rosalyn reached down in her bag and pulled out the notebook she'd begged him to let her keep. She turned to an entry. "It said 'If you like Steve so much, I guess I'll need to meet him soon.'" She closed the notebook and laid it in her lap.

Steve's hands gripped the steering wheel tighter. "When did this note arrive? What time?"

"At around three o'clock in the morning. You were asleep. I heard it slide under the door."

The Watcher had been at his door. For him to have been so close and Steve to have known nothing about it infuriated him. "So you opened it, right? When you saw what it was, why didn't you wake me up?"

He understood why Rosalyn wouldn't run after a stalker, but Steve wouldn't have any qualms whatsoever about doing so.

She stared at him for a long minute. "I thought you were some businessman. I had no idea you were in law enforcement."

"I didn't have to be in law enforcement to help you. Any decent human being would've wanted to help you deal with a maniac who was tracking your every move."

"I had already lost two decent human beings for that very reason! I couldn't go through that again. Couldn't drag you into my own personal hell."

Steve gritted his teeth. Logically he could understand why she hadn't wanted to tell him about the Watcher, but he still wished she had. This could've already been settled by now.

"Two? Someone else tried to help you? What happened?"

"A mechanic in Memphis named Shawn. It was before I knew better. And certainly before I knew he had some sort of bug transmitting everything I said."

"He died?"

Rosalyn nodded. "The night I told him about the Watcher."

"Another heart attack, like the detective?"

"No. The news called it a random act of violence. Some sort of gang retaliation, even though the guy had never been involved with gangs and wasn't even near that part of town." Rosalyn turned toward the window. "So no, I wasn't about to tell you about the Watcher and see you die also."

She'd carried a lot of weight by herself for many months, having to worry about not only herself but other people too. And now a baby. Most people would've buckled under the pressure.

He redirected the conversation. "But you haven't heard anything from the Watcher since that night at the hotel when we were together?"

"Well, once I got back to Pensacola three days ago to meet my sister, I heard from him. Another note under my hotel room door." She shuddered.

"This one was worse than the others?"

"No, it had just been so long since I'd received anything."

"So you mean after the morning you left me six months ago, you hadn't heard from the Watcher until you came back to Pensacola this week?"

That meant something. Steve didn't know exactly what yet, but he knew that the Watcher's absence from Rosalyn's life for six months would be a big clue in solving the case.

"Where did you go when you left me?"

She looked over at him and flushed. "I'm sorry I stole your money. I didn't have any left."

"I would've given it to you if you'd asked."

"That would've involved giving you more information than was good for your health."

"I would've preferred that to waking up with you gone and thinking the worst of you for six months."

Actually, he'd thought worse of himself than her. That he'd been a gullible fool. But he'd thought pretty badly of her too.

That wasn't what was important now. "So you took nearly $200…"

"You have to understand, I was at a pretty low place. Everywhere I'd gone, the Watcher had found me. Admittedly, he hadn't tried to hurt me like he has this week, but it was still wearing me down. A note slipped under my door every night or so, knowing he was that close…"

"I'm sure it was nerve-racking."

"It was nerve-racking the first couple of months. By the time I met you, I was considering just killing myself and saving the Watcher the trouble."

He glanced over at her. "Seriously?"

She nodded. "That night at the bar when we met, I ran in because of the rain. I'd been out watching the sunset, considering if taking my own life would be better than letting the Watcher continue to kill innocent people."

Steve couldn't even bear to think about it. "Rosalyn—"

"Then I met you," she continued. "It didn't change anything really, but—"

She stopped and looked away.

"But what?"

"I connected with someone. With you. It was the first time I hadn't felt alone in so long." She tucked a strand of hair behind her ear. "I wasn't using you for money, Steve. I panicked when I saw the Watcher's note. All I could think of was getting away."

He believed her. She hadn't taken his credit cards or stolen his rental car. If she'd been trying to take him for all she could, she wouldn't have left those behind.

"Okay, so what did you do when you left that morning?"

"I took a bus as far as the money I stole from you would take me. I didn't want to go back to my car—I just wanted to get out of town. That ended up being Ellijay, Georgia."

"Never heard of it."

"I'd be shocked if you had. It's a tiny town north of Atlanta, in the Blue Ridge Mountains. Population just over fifteen hundred."

"What was in Ellijay?"

"Nothing whatsoever. That's just where my money ran out."

She stared out the window for a long time.

"Did Ellijay end up being good or bad?"

"Good. Definitely good. I needed to get some money right away, so I asked the couple who owned the small café in town if I could wash dishes or do any odd jobs just for the day, for cash.

"Mr. and Mrs. Ammons—Jim and Cheryl—said yes. I washed dishes a couple of days and didn't really have anywhere to go."

Steve's teeth gritted but he didn't say anything.

"Cheryl invited me to stay at their house, which was above the café. I slept in their son's room. He had died in the army a long time ago."

"And you had no notes or communication with the Watcher the whole time?"

"Nothing. I thought maybe he'd moved on or I was out of the territory he considered 'his.'" She shrugged. "Or maybe he had followed me but once he saw I was pregnant, I no longer interested him."

Any of those scenarios were possible.

"I definitely didn't tell the Ammonses about him," Rosalyn continued, shifting on the seat to get comfortable. "I didn't want to take a chance with their lives. Plus, Jim was already pretty paranoid since their son died due to a military communication breach or something. Jim and Cheryl live completely off the grid. No cell phone, no television, no computers or internet."

"I'm glad you had someone to help you."

"They're amazing. Gruff and not very talkative, and pretty old-fashioned. When I found out I was pregnant, I was afraid they might turn me out, but they didn't even think about it."

"Why did you leave? If the Watcher had lost track of you, why didn't you just stay in Ellijay?"

From the corner of his eye he could see Rosalyn's hands begin twisting in her lap. "As I was getting further and further along in my pregnancy, I began to think about the future. To worry that the Watcher was playing some sort of game. That maybe he was waiting until the baby was born and then would take me or both of us.

"I like the Ammonses a lot, but they're older, in their seventies. They couldn't take care of a baby. So I decided to call Lindsey. To just meet with her and see what shape her life was in."

She glanced at him, then out the window quickly. Obviously there was more to the story.

"And?"

"And what?"

"And what are you trying to get away with not telling me?"

"Nothing. It's not important."

"Rosalyn, anything having to do with you and the baby is important."

She shrugged. "I had Lindsey meet me in Pensacola because I was going to try to talk the hotel into giving me your info so I could contact you."

"For what, money?" As soon as the words were out of his mouth, Steve wished he could cut off his own tongue.

Rosalyn didn't look at him, just shifted her weight so her back was to him and she was looking completely out the window.

"I'm sorry. I didn't mean that." He wished he could see her face.

"Yes, you did. At least part of you did. The part of you who knows me as someone who lied, stole from you, then showed up pregnant with what may or may not be your baby. The part of you who doesn't want to be taken in again."

"Rosalyn—"

"You know what? I don't even blame you. You're right to be wary. Hopefully that will keep you alive longer."

Steve tried to figure out how to undo the damage his words had done.

She laid her seat back, still facing away from him. "We've got a long drive ahead. If you don't mind, I'm going to rest now so I can take a driving shift later. It'll make it easier on everyone."

He wasn't sure if she meant sleeping now would make it easier or driving later would do so. Clarifying would just make it worse, so he decided to let it go.

He knew she hadn't been coming to find him for money. For physical security, yes, but not money.

He shouldn't have said what he had. Even if he did still mistrust her. She hadn't given him much reason to trust her, truth be told.

Some of that he could alleviate right now. He knew Rosalyn was asleep, so he called his office.

"Cynthia," he said to his assistant by way of greeting. "I need everything you can give me about Rosalyn Mellinger. And anything you can find on Jim and Cheryl Ammons. North Georgia."

"Got it."

"I'll need you to call me back and read it to me. There's been a change of plans. We're driving from Pensacola back to HQ."

"That's quite a trek."

"Couldn't stay in Pensacola any longer. Had two attempts on our lives in under twelve hours." Steve explained about the driver and fire.

"Damn, boss. Do you want me to redirect an Omega plane to you? Or send Liam or one of the guys out to meet you for protection?"

"No, I got rid of how he was tracking us. We should be fine now. We'll stop at a hotel tonight, but I should be in the office by tomorrow afternoon."

"I'll make sure Joe has all the party paraphernalia gone by then."

Steve snickered. Joe Matarazzo was the team's hostage negotiator and was known for his partying. Or had been until his wife, Laura, reined him in a few months ago.

Rosalyn hadn't budged during his entire conversation. Her breathing hadn't changed; there'd been no sudden tension to make him think she was awake. She was exhausted. She'd barely gotten any sleep before the fire had awakened them again.

She was still sound asleep two hours later when Jon Hatton, one of Omega's best profilers and Steve's personal friend, called him back.

"Hey, boss, Cynthia and I have been gathering the info you wanted."

"Anything interesting?"

"Rosalyn Mellinger, twenty-four years old. Daughter of Crystal Mellinger and twin sister to Lindsey Rose. Hey, I see what the mom did there with the names—"

"Yeah, already got that, Jon. Keep going."

"No father listed on the birth certificate. Arrested as a teenager for shoplifting. That's where her prints are from and that sealed juvenile record was a bitch to get opened. But that little run-in with the law must have scared her straight because she's been straight as an arrow as an adult. Went to college, became an accountant. Worked every day until the day she quit. Not even a parking ticket."

Steve glanced over at Rosalyn, still asleep. "Okay."

"Sister has been in and out of juvie rehabs, then adult versions since her mid-teens. No college, barely finished high school. The mom is pretty much a deadbeat also. Alcoholic. Lives on welfare."

Okay, so no family support for Rosalyn. That explained why she'd been on the run by herself for a year.

"In the last few months Rosalyn's name has been mentioned in multiple police reports, all over the

Southeast and Texas. She's been talking to them about a stalker, but nothing has come of any of the investigations. Nobody has been taking her seriously."

"Well, I'm taking her seriously now, Jon. Someone nearly killed us twice in the last day."

"I'll see what I can dig up on the reports."

"Thanks, Jon. And if you can find out all you can about a Detective Johnson in Shreveport—he would've died of a heart attack eight or nine months ago—and a mechanic in Memphis who was killed in a random act of gang violence. Shawn something."

"Okay, these two related?"

"Just look for anything suspicious in either."

"All right, and we're still checking on the Ammonses. All I can find so far is a dead son in the military nearly fifteen years ago. They keep a low profile, whoever they are. I can't even find a bank account."

"That fits with what Rosalyn told me. Let me know if there's anything else."

"Got it. You watch your six, boss. I've already got a hinky feeling about this whole thing."

Steve took Jon's "hinky" feelings very seriously. Not to mention, Steve felt like they were dealing with something pretty major too. He said his goodbyes and disconnected the call.

Rosalyn turned in her sleep toward him, obviously finding it difficult to get comfortable. He had thought about driving all the way through the night and getting to Colorado Springs in one push.

But that wouldn't work. Rosalyn needed a bed where she could get a proper night's rest. Somewhere where no one was trying to run her over or set the building on fire or slipping notes under her door.

Rosalyn had been on her own for way too long. Steve planned to show her she wasn't alone anymore.

Chapter Eleven

She awoke to Steve's voice again, but at least this time he wasn't trying to tell her the building was on fire.

"Let's get you inside. Then you can go back to sleep if you want."

She looked at the handsome man, so strong and able, who had her tucked into his side leading her into the hotel lobby. Oh, she wanted, but sleep wasn't it.

She wanted him. Sometimes he said stupid stuff, but she still wanted him.

He used the key card to enter their room and turned on the light. This was a much nicer room than the ones she'd slept in for the last year when she hadn't been at the Ammonses' house. Generic, sure, but clean, tasteful, new. With a king-size bed in the middle of it.

She walked all the way in, then turned to him. "No hot tub this time."

She almost smiled at the speed with which his eyes flew to hers. Good. She wasn't the only one affected by the heat between them.

"Yeah, a shame." He pulled himself together and turned to close the door behind them. "Sorry we don't have any change of clothes. Once we get to Colorado Springs, I'll make sure you get something right away."

"It's no problem. I'm sure I'll be okay for one more day in these."

Maybe it was the fact that she'd slept most of the day or maybe it was because Steve had found the electronic transmitters and that just explained so damn much, but Rosalyn felt different.

For the first time since this nightmare began nearly a year ago, she was positive there would not be a note under the door tonight.

All those times she thought she was crazy, that the Watcher could hear her thoughts, that he lived inside her head? He'd simply lived inside the fiber of her clothing, able to hear who she'd talked to, where she'd checked in. That's how he'd found her.

All the times Rosalyn had talked to herself, he'd been privy to those conversations. Embarrassing, but at least it all made sense now.

The fact that he had gotten close enough to put transmitters on her clothing was terrifying. Steve had found two. Who knew how many more there might have been in the clothing that had been destroyed by the fire.

But there weren't any transmitters anymore. Rosalyn didn't even mind the ill-fitting supermarket clothes she was wearing now, because it meant nobody could hear her. Nobody but she and Steve knew where they were.

She hadn't realized how much weight she had shouldered for so long until a great deal of it was lifted. It allowed her to focus on other things.

Like how she was in a hotel with a gorgeous man. Six feet of muscle and awareness. Dark hair and green eyes staring at her like he was slightly nervous about what she would do next.

She hadn't had anyone but him hold her in the last year. No one had kissed her or pulled her into any embrace at all except for Steve. No one had touched her.

Sure, Jim and Cheryl Ammons had given her a brush on the shoulder or pat on the back here and there. Physical demonstration of affection wasn't the older couple's way. They weren't heartless, and cared about her for sure, but they just weren't very demonstrative in showing it.

It wasn't like she missed it. Rosalyn had been raised in a house where affectionate touches were few and far between. It was one of the things she'd promised herself her child would never go without. Her son would be hugged and kissed until he squirmed to get away. He would know every day he was loved, not just by words but by gestures.

But watching Steve cross the room, secure the door to make sure they were safe and turn those intense green eyes back on her, Rosalyn was quite sure of the type of touch *she* wanted right now.

And a hug wasn't it.

She wasn't looking for comfort, like she had been six months ago. She wanted the heat she and Steve had felt together.

He slowly took a step toward her. She smiled at his hesitancy. The cop in him must be aware of the predator in the room.

Her.

And he was the prey. Big, strong sexy man probably wasn't used to that.

"Do you want to take a shower first or do you want me to?" he asked.

"What about taking one together?"

"Rosalyn…" His words were a protest, but she saw the tightening of his body. The slight flare in his eyes.

She took a step toward him. "We'll at least save water that way."

"I have a feeling we'd be in there too long to save any water." He tried to step around her so he could get to the other side of the room, but she moved so she was right in front of him.

"So take a shower with me and don't save water."

She could almost see his conscience pour over him. "Rosalyn, it's been a really long couple of days. Traumatic couple of days."

The words were for her benefit, not his. She raised one eyebrow and gave him a little snicker. "And you're tired? Need a little you time? Drink a chai latte or something?"

She saw the smile he fought against. He wanted her—she knew he did. She wasn't going to give up at his first token protest.

"No, I'm talking about you. You've had a rough couple of days, hell, a rough few months. There's no need to jump into anything just because you're relieved or grateful or whatever."

"Generally I don't pay my debts with sex, if that's what you're thinking."

He winced. "No, I didn't mean you were trying to pay me. I just meant—"

She stepped closer to stop him from saying anything further. He was digging himself a hole and she was afraid he was going to piss her off with whatever asinine thing came out of his mouth next.

"Steve, don't overthink it."

"Somebody needs to overthink it. Or at least think at all."

He was protective of her and she appreciated that. But right now she didn't want him to use his strength to protect her. She wanted him to use his strength to help her celebrate how good it felt to be unfettered for the first time in as long as she could remember.

She ran both her hands up his arms. She felt him tense but he didn't pull away. She leaned in closer.

"I'm happy to be alive. I'm happy no one is going to find me and slip a note under the door tonight. I'm happy we're both safe here together."

She slid her arms to his shoulders, then around his neck, pulling his lips down to hers.

The heat was still there. Thank goodness it wasn't just something she'd remembered, something she'd dreamed about. His lips were still as firm and hot and inviting as she'd known they would be.

But he wasn't pulling her to him. His hands were on her waist, but they seemed neutral—neither encouraging nor discouraging.

"Rosalyn..." he groaned against her mouth.

He was going to let her go, she could tell.

"Steve, you got me away from a lunatic. I want to celebrate that."

Those were the wrong words. He stepped back from her. "You don't owe me anything."

Were they really back to that again? "I know. And I appreciate very much that you're not the type of guy who would try to lord that over my head. But that's not the point."

He grabbed her arms and set her back from him. "Look, I've worked around people who have been traumatized by violence. Sometimes it's hard to recognize the symptoms in yourself. I just don't want you to do something you might regret."

Rosalyn smiled. She appreciated his concern, she really did. But this wasn't something she was going to regret—she was positive about that. "Believe me, I'm not going to regret this."

She tried to step forward but he stopped her.

"Well, have you considered that maybe I don't want to do this? That it's something I'll regret?" Frustration flavored his tone.

He didn't want her. The reality hit her like a bucket of ice. She immediately stepped back from him.

What did she expect, really? She'd lied to him, stolen from him, dragged him into a situation that had almost gotten him killed twice. Not to mention shown up pregnant with his baby.

Of course getting involved with her physically wasn't a good idea for him. Yeah, there was heat between them, but he was smart enough to know that wasn't enough to justify getting close to her.

All the perk, all the joy seemed to drain out of her. "You're right—I hadn't thought of that. Smart move on your part."

"Rosalyn…" He took a step toward her.

She immediately jerked back. He couldn't touch her.

Not now. If he did, she might shatter into a million pieces. "I'm going to take a shower."

She turned and all but ran.

STEVE WATCHED ROSALYN nearly run across the room to the bathroom.

Damn it. What the hell was the matter with him? Why would he say that to her?

He was the director of one of the most prestigious law enforcement agencies in the country. He regularly spoke to the congressmen, senators, the president's advisers. Hell, he'd even spoken to two different presidents in his tenure as the director of the Critical Response Division.

He was known for being well-spoken. Known for reading a situation and doing and/or saying whatever was needed. He had a team of dozens of people who looked to him to provide guidance and leadership. To know the words that needed to be said when everything around them was falling apart.

Yet somehow he'd just managed to say the worst possible thing to one small, fragile woman who'd just been reaching out to him for human contact.

And the worst thing about his ridiculous words? None of them were true.

Not want her? That was so far from the truth he could barely wrap his mind around it.

But he was convinced she felt beholden to him. That she wouldn't really want him under normal circumstances that didn't involve life-threatening situations.

Of course, he wanted her pretty desperately, and life-threatening situations were commonplace for him.

His fingers itched to touch her. To run through her hair and along her body. To see the changes pregnancy had made, beyond what he could make out from beneath her clothes.

He wanted her with a passion that went against everything in his calm, collected nature. He couldn't ever remember wanting anyone this much. Not even his wife, Melanie. They'd loved each other, absolutely, but with the low simmer of the knowledge that they would have the rest of their lives together to work through their love.

The rest of their lives together had ended up being only six short years.

The fire that consumed him every time he was around Rosalyn was so different from that it almost couldn't be compared. Being around her caused him to lose his cool. Lose his focus.

Melanie would approve. Deep in the back of his mind, Steve knew his wife would approve of the young woman in the bathroom who had stayed alive under some pretty desperate circumstances. Would approve of the fact that Rosalyn shook him up enough to make him say stupid things.

He heard the shower turn on in the bathroom.

And maybe Rosalyn just wanted him because she wanted him. Not because of anything else but this damn heat between them. An itch that had just barely gotten scratched six months ago and had been driving them both crazy ever since.

Maybe he'd just sent her running despondent into

the bathroom not because he didn't want her—he almost laughed outright at the thought—but because of some ridiculous, completely wrong feeling of over-protection.

He was an idiot.

The bathroom door opened but her head didn't pop out. "You know what, Drackett? You're an idiot."

His legs were moving before his brain had even processed what was going on. He caught the bathroom door just before it shut and pushed it all the way open.

Rosalyn's mouth made a little o.

But the heat burned in her eyes the way he knew it burned in his.

"You know what? I *am* an idiot."

He kissed her.

There was no gentleness in the kiss. No finesse.

But there was plenty of heat and need and passion.

He lifted her up and set her on the bathroom vanity, then grabbed her hips and slid her all the way to the edge until she was flush up against him. They both groaned as her calves hooked around the backs of his thighs. Her fingers linked behind his neck, keeping him against her.

"Rosalyn, I'm sorry—" He began his murmured apology against her mouth, but she stopped him.

"No apologies. No talking. No thinking."

He couldn't hide the effect she had on him, didn't even try to pretend he could control his response. He just let the heat take over.

As he stripped them both out of their clothes and slipped his arms around her hips to carry her with him to the shower—unwilling to separate their bodies for even the few steps it would take for them to walk—he hoped the heat consuming them both wouldn't burn them away.

Leaving nothing but ash in its place.

Chapter Twelve

They got on the road again early, after catching a quick breakfast. By lunch they were only a few hours from Colorado Springs. They stopped at a truck-stop diner just outside Dalhart, Texas, off Highway 87.

Rosalyn felt rested. She shouldn't, since she'd been awake for a big chunk of the night for the best of reasons, but she did.

Steve had seemed fascinated by the changes in her body that had come about from the pregnancy. She was right at the perfect stage: not sick and tired all the time like she'd been in the early days, but not so big that she was waddling around. She knew that would be coming soon.

There were a lot of things unsettled about her future. What was she going to do when she got to Colorado Springs? Get a job and stay there? She had some money she'd saved from working at the diner, but not enough. Especially not when the baby came.

Another thing she and Steve needed to talk about. The list was getting pretty long.

She was concerned about the future but for the first time the thought didn't send her into a near panic.

Maybe it was the knowledge that the Watcher could no longer find her now that the transmitting devices in her clothes were gone. Maybe it was because Steve was here and believed she was in danger.

But she had slept like she hadn't been able to sleep in months. Even when she'd been at the Ammonses' house and it seemed liked the Watcher couldn't find her, she hadn't slept this good.

She was sure having Steve's arms around her helped.

But even if they hadn't made love, if he hadn't held her, she knew just his presence made a huge difference to her psyche. She wasn't alone. And although there was a lot she and Steve still needed to work out, she knew it would happen eventually.

He was looking through her notebook now, the one with all the dates and recordings of the notes or messages the Watcher had given her.

"I wish we hadn't lost all the notes in the fire." She sipped on her iced tea, knowing she shouldn't be drinking caffeine, but surely one cup wouldn't hurt. She savored it as well as her large lunch.

Steve shrugged. "They would've helped for sure, especially with prosecution for stalking. But this notebook gives us a lot of information. My people will be able to see what patterns can be established from this."

"Detective Johnson steered me right by telling me to write everything down. Actually, at the time, I think he just told me that to give me something proactive to do. Make me feel less like a victim, more like an active part in an investigation."

And it had worked. For the first time Rosalyn had

felt hopeful. Right up until Johnson had died two days later.

Steve took her hand. "I already have people looking into his death and the mechanic's. They'll dig through what it looks like on the surface to what's actually underneath, okay?"

Rosalyn nodded. "Thank you."

He handed the notebook back to her. "I'm going to pay and use the restroom. Then we'll hit the road again. We should make it to Colorado Springs by this afternoon."

She smiled. "I'll try not to sleep the entire day away this time."

He stood up. "You can do whatever you need to— don't worry about that. It's been a stressful couple of days. Your body needs rest."

It had been a stressful year. But she just nodded.

She was thankful Steve was looking into Detective Johnson's and Shawn the mechanic's deaths. She still didn't know exactly what Steve did in law enforcement, but evidently he was pretty high up. He hadn't offered any information and she hadn't wanted to ask.

She needed to call the Ammonses before they got back on the road. She needed to let them know she was okay. They didn't have a phone upstairs at their house, due mostly to Jim's paranoia that the government was listening or watching them, but had one at the café.

Rosalyn got change from the waitress and went into the hallway lined with phones, a throwback from before everyone had cell phones and truckers used to have to make calls to their loved ones from pay phones. She dialed the number for the Ammonses' café, then put in the change required to connect the call.

"Main Street Cafe."

"Hi, Cheryl, it's—"

"Oh, Rosalyn, honey! Thank goodness you're okay."

It was the most emotion she'd ever heard out of the stoic Cheryl.

"I'm sorry if you've been worried about me. I should've called earlier."

But a deranged stalker found me again, killed my sister, then tried to kill me twice.

Rosalyn had never told the Ammonses about the Watcher. She suspected they knew she was on the run from someone but had never pressed for details and she'd never given any.

"That's all right. I'm just glad to hear you're safe now. Jim was worried too."

Rosalyn laughed. "I don't think Jim worries about anything but the government encroaching on his boundaries."

"Well, he talked yesterday about putting a phone line in the house so you could call there if you needed anything."

Rosalyn felt tears come to her eyes. For Jim to have considered that, he really did care about her. "Cheryl, I'll just call the café, okay? Tell Jim he doesn't need to do anything so drastic like get a phone in the house."

The words were in jest, but Rosalyn meant it. She knew what it meant for Jim to have even considered it.

"Are you coming back? You know you're welcome anytime. You and the baby."

"Thanks, Cheryl." Emotion choked Rosalyn's voice.

"I've got some things to take care of. But I might be back. I don't know yet."

"Well, we both mean it when we say we want you here. Don't forget that, okay?"

"Yes, ma'am. I'm with the baby's father now and we're trying to get some stuff figured out." Probably not the stuff Cheryl was thinking of, but that didn't matter. "I'll call in a couple of days with an update, okay?"

"You be careful, hon. And remember you've always got a home here if you want it."

"Thanks, Cheryl. Give Jim my love."

"I will. Bye."

Rosalyn put the phone receiver back in its cradle and leaned her head against it. It was nice to know she had someone who cared about her. That she had options. But she wondered if she was opening up the Ammonses to the Watcher's clutches. What if he found her again? If she went back there, would she be leading him to them? She couldn't stand the thought of the older couple falling victim to him.

Maybe she'd done the wrong thing by calling them at all. But surely with the transmitters gone, no harm would come to them.

She looked up to find Steve staring at her, eyes narrowed. She gave him a little wave as he walked over, but all the easy camaraderie they'd had at lunch, the closeness they'd shared last night seemed to be gone.

"I would've let you use my phone if you needed to make a call. You didn't have to pay for it."

"That's okay. I didn't want to bother you. And I didn't want to waste time. I know we're trying to make it to Colorado Springs as quickly as we can."

Rosalyn was still a little overcome with emotion after talking to Cheryl. It must be pregnancy hormones or something. But the thought of Jim agreeing to put a phone in his house just because of her had tears rushing to her eyes again. She turned away so Steve wouldn't see.

"Ready to go?" she asked.

Steve grabbed her arm. "Who were you talking to, Rosalyn?"

The anger behind the words took her aback. "Who do you think I was talking to?"

"I don't know. All I know is I leave you alone for the first time in twenty-four hours and you're making mysterious phone calls."

"I was calling Cheryl and Jim Ammons. The people in Ellijay with whom I had been staying. I wanted to let them know I was all right."

"And you couldn't wait to do that in the car on my phone?"

He was still holding her arm. Rosalyn snatched it away. "I didn't think of that, okay? I've been on my own for a while now and I'm not used to having other people around or their resources."

Steve's eyes narrowed more, so she turned and walked out toward the car. Let him believe whatever he wanted to.

It was going to be a long ride to Colorado Springs.

THE HOURS ON the way to Colorado Springs were tense at best. Rosalyn never told him exactly who she had been contacting, but he didn't believe her when she said it was the Ammonses, the couple in Ellijay who had taken her in. After all, hadn't she already told him the husband didn't trust the government and they lived off the grid?

No computer, no phone. So how exactly had she called them?

Steve didn't want to let it, especially after last night, but true doubt about Rosalyn crept in. He was trained to see evil in innocent actions, to question all possibilities.

He had to face the fact that Rosalyn could be using him right now. That she had initiated contact with him in Pensacola for a particular purpose that had nothing to do with the baby or the Watcher.

To what end, he didn't exactly know. But he had to admit she could be working with some sort of partner to get something from him or maneuver him in some way. Maybe she knew who he really was in Omega. He had access to top secret information on a regular basis. Maybe she was hoping to obtain something through him.

He just couldn't get out of his mind how sad she'd looked when getting off the phone. How guilty.

Like she'd done something distasteful and wished she could take it back.

Why would she feel that way after talking to a couple she'd been close to for half a year? And for that matter, why wouldn't she just have used his phone to contact them? It would've made a lot more sense.

Or was it just like Rosalyn had said? She wasn't used to depending on other people. She hadn't had a cell phone in a while. Maybe she hadn't even considered it. She'd just seen the pay phone—a rarity these days—and decided to make the call while Steve was doing other things.

Certainly not nefarious when thought of that way.

Steve's hands gripped the steering wheel tighter. It wasn't often that he called his own judgments and gut feelings into question.

But when it came to Rosalyn, he had to admit that he was not neutral.

He decided to try to talk to her. They couldn't spend the rest of the five hours in silence.

"I'm going to take you into my office. I have people looking into your situation."

She nodded. "Okay. You still haven't told me exactly what you do or who you work for."

He didn't answer. Was it interesting that she would be pressing for info on that topic now or was he just reading into things that weren't there? He looked over at Rosalyn, her crystal-blue eyes staring at him.

He'd swear she was guileless. But he couldn't take the risk. The Critical Response Division wasn't one of the covert divisions of Omega, but Steve still couldn't take a chance on giving Rosalyn any information if he suspected she was working with someone.

God, what a mess that was going to be if she was. Because what if a paternity test proved the baby was his but Rosalyn was really in cahoots with a criminal?

Complicated was an understatement.

Chapter Thirteen

Great. She was trapped in the car with Broody McScary.

What had happened to the passionate man she'd made love with last night? He been here with her until they'd eaten lunch.

Maybe he had indigestion.

No, it wasn't lunch. It was her phone call. He didn't like that she'd had a conversation he couldn't hear. It didn't take a genius to figure out why.

He didn't trust her.

She didn't know exactly what bad thing he kept expecting her to do. Hell, she didn't think *he* knew what bad thing he expected her to do. But obviously he expected something.

She didn't even really want to talk to him, and avoided doing so by pretending to sleep part of the way. But about an hour outside Colorado Springs, she had to go to the bathroom.

"Can we make one short pit stop?"

"We've got less than an hour. We're almost to Pueblo. Can't you hold it?"

If he'd been annoyed, she would've argued with him. But he didn't look annoyed. He looked distrustful.

"Fine." She would hold it, even if it killed her.

Thirty minutes later she was afraid it really would.

"Look, we're going to have to stop, okay? I know you think I'm planning some sort of nuclear attack or whatever, but my pregnant body is not going to wait to go to the bathroom."

He almost cracked a smile at that. "Fine. I'll get gas while we stop."

He pulled up at the gas pump and Rosalyn ran inside to use the restroom. She felt much better when she came back out. She wondered what she could do to help ease the tension between her and Steve. She had to accept it was his job to be distrustful—he was a cop, after all. She shouldn't be offended if he was butting into her business with questions all the time. Especially if it was because he was trying to keep her safe.

She would be the better person. Maybe buy him a candy bar as a peace offering. Who could resist chocolate? Plus, she was hungry.

Then again, she was always hungry.

She looked out the gas-station convenience-store window at Steve, wondering what he would like. A guy on a motorcycle was moving slowly toward Steve as he pumped the gas. Steve was looking at her. Probably to make sure she wasn't robbing the cash register.

At first she didn't pay any mind to the motorcycle except to wonder why he was coming up directly behind their car rather than to one of the empty pumps. But then she saw the rider pull something out of his jacket. It looked like a small stick.

Then he flicked his wrist and it grew into a much longer club.

He was going to hit Steve with it.

Rosalyn dropped the candy and ran toward the door knowing there was no way she'd make it outside in time to warn Steve or stop the motorcycle guy.

Something in her face alerted him, or maybe just his cop instincts, and he spun and threw up his arm just as the club came at his head.

A soft scream came out of her mouth as she saw the impact. It had to have hurt—had maybe even broken his arm—but at least Steve was still on his feet. A blow that severe to his head would've killed him.

In the corner of her mind the agony of what this meant—the Watcher had found her again—tried to take control, but she wouldn't let it. She couldn't have a breakdown right now. She had to help Steve.

"Call the police!" she yelled at the cashier. "My friend is being attacked."

She didn't wait to see if the cashier did it; she just ran through the doors.

The guy pulled the club back for another swing, but Steve was more prepared this time. The attacker swung from the side rather than in a downward motion and Steve ducked. He brought his uninjured arm up like he planned to use it to punch the guy, but the man was too far away for Steve to be able to reach him. The stick gave him all the advantage.

He brought it down at Steve again, with not as much force, but it still knocked Steve to the ground as it hit his shoulder. He got back up, but the attacker was already bringing his arm around again.

"Hey, leave him alone!" Rosalyn didn't think through the wisdom of being unarmed, smaller and pregnant when facing the attacker, just knew she had to get him away from Steve. The best way to do that would be to bring as much attention to the situation as possible.

The motorcycle man looked at her, but she couldn't see his face through the darkened visor.

"Yeah, you, get away from him. Somebody help us!"

Rosalyn might not be able to do much but she could scream her head off. She also reached for bottles of oil that were stacked by the front door as she ran past them, throwing them as she went. None of them got far enough to hit the attacker, but at least she was making enough of a spectacle of herself to draw even more attention.

Other people were coming out of the store and a car on the road had pulled in to see what was going on. The motorcycle man realized the situation and threw his stick down and sped off. Nobody could do anything to stop him.

Rosalyn ran over to Steve.

"Are you okay?"

He was still cradling the arm he'd used to block the first—and hardest—hit. "Yeah. I'm okay. I don't have much feeling in my arm, but better than if he had hit me in the head."

Rosalyn clenched her teeth to keep them from chattering at the thought. "It would've killed you."

"Probably not. But it definitely would've knocked me unconscious long enough for him to finish the job."

They heard sirens heading toward them.

"I told the clerk to call the cops. I didn't know what else to do."

Steve tilted his head sideways and looked at her. "You had the clerk call the police?"

"Yeah, well, I wasn't sure my oilcan throwing was going to stop the motorcycle guy, so I thought we better get reinforcements here as soon as possible. Is your arm okay? Let me look at it."

She took a step toward him but stopped when he backed up. She tried not to let his actions hurt her feelings. It probably wasn't personal. He was in pain. Trying to figure out what had happened. Cop mode.

It wasn't long before two police cars and an ambulance were pulling up.

"Do you mind waiting by the car?" Steve asked. "It'll be less complicated if I talk to the locals alone at first."

"Yeah, okay." She shrugged. "I'll be over at the car."

A paramedic walked up to them before she went, so Rosalyn waited. She wanted to make sure Steve was okay.

"Ma'am, were you hurt in any way?" the paramedic asked her.

"No. I was in the store, nowhere near the guy with his club."

"Guy on a motorcycle came up, had an expandable baton." Steve began rolling up his sleeve so he could show his injuries to the paramedic.

Rosalyn gasped when she saw his forearm. It was swollen and already turning purple.

The medic took Steve's arm in his hand. "Can you move all your fingers without pain?"

Steve wiggled them. "Nothing sharp. Just an all-over ache."

The medic probed gently around the bruise. "It doesn't seem to be broken, but you should probably get it x-rayed to be sure. You're fortunate. Whoever did this was trying to do you serious harm. It could've shattered your arm."

Steve nodded. "It could've done much worse if he had gotten me on the skull like he was aiming for."

The medic whistled through his teeth. "Yes, for sure. Do you have any other injuries?"

"He got me across the shoulders also, but not with nearly as much force." Steve turned so the medic could see.

"You'll want to get these photographed so it can be used against whoever did this when they catch him," the medic said. "But beyond that, there's no reason for you to come with me. You'll probably be hurting pretty bad for a few days."

"Thanks. I'll take care of it." Steve turned to her. "I'm going to talk to the officer. You stay right at the car, okay?"

Rosalyn nodded and walked over to lean against the trunk. Steve went to talk to the two officers who had shown up, turning so he was facing her. She saw him pull out some sort of badge or ID and show it to the officers.

Now that she was alone and not worried for Steve's immediate well-being, the weight of what had just happened hit her.

The Watcher had found her again.

There was no way this incident could be a coincidence. But how? They had left all the clothes, with the electronic transmitters, in that superstore dressing room. The only thing she'd kept had been her notebook.

And she'd searched every single sheet of paper in it during the car ride. There had been absolutely nothing unusual.

She didn't know how he had found her, only that he had. And Steve had almost paid the price for it right before her eyes.

Maybe she should run. Right now. Maybe if she left and got away from Steve, the Watcher would leave him alone.

She turned and put her elbows against the passenger-side window, cradling her head in her hands. What was she going to do? She was going to have the baby soon. She couldn't keep running forever.

Especially since running didn't seem to matter. The Watcher found her no matter where she went. The only place he hadn't found her was at the Ammonses' house. Or if he had, he'd never made his presence known.

Rosalyn turned and glanced at Steve. He was still talking to the officers, but he was looking at her. One of the men nodded at whatever Steve was saying and looked at Rosalyn too. The other gave something to Steve that he put in his pocket. Steve shook hands with both men again and began walking toward the car.

"You seem pretty upset. Are you okay?" he asked her.

Rosalyn laughed, but there was no humor in the sound. Was she okay? No. She wasn't certain she was ever going to be okay. "No, I'm definitely not okay."

"Why? Because he didn't succeed or because you changed your mind?"

She studied his face more carefully. His green eyes were cold. The angles of his jaw set in anger.

"What?"

"I saw you looking at the guy on the motorcycle. You were looking at both of us right before he hit me."

She shook her head, trying to process exactly what Steve was implying. "Yeah, I noticed him, but I didn't think anything of it."

He took a step closer to her, his height intimidating rather than comforting. "Why were you studying me so intensely from inside the convenience store, then?"

"I was trying to figure out which candy bar to get you." Her words were small. They sounded ridiculous even to her own ears.

"You called someone earlier, someone you didn't want me to know about. Was that him? The Watcher? Are you working together?"

Rosalyn could feel the blood leaving her face. "Wh-what?"

He grabbed her arm with his good hand. "Did you decide you didn't want me dead at the last minute? Did you change your mind? Is that why you made that horrified face in the store and tipped me off?"

"I made the face because I saw he was going to hit you—"

"Which was the plan all along, right? Except you had some sort of change of heart and decided to tip me off. If you hadn't made that face, I have to admit, I'd be dead now."

She couldn't believe what she was hearing. "No. No, I didn't know what he was going to do until he flicked out that stick thing—"

"Really? You expect me to believe he just happened to find us right after you just happened to make a secret call at lunch today? Is that why you had me stop here when we were so close to Colorado Springs?"

"No. Steve, I—"

He took a step back. "You know what? Save it. We'll do official questioning when I get you into the Critical Response office."

"The what?"

He didn't answer. Instead he pulled a set of handcuffs out of his pocket. That's what the officer had handed him. Rosalyn looked over at them. They were watching her and Steve. Evidently he had already told them why he would need the handcuffs.

Almost as if from a distance, she felt a cuff slip around one wrist, then the other.

"Rosalyn Mellinger, you're under arrest."

Chapter Fourteen

She was playing him. Had to have been this entire time. There was no other explanation for it.

Steve could feel the anger coursing through his body. Not just at Rosalyn, although he was plenty pissed at her, but at himself also.

She'd taken him as an easy mark once, six months ago, and obviously had found he was still just as dense even after being fooled by her before.

Even worse? He still wanted to believe her now. That the crushed look on her face was real, that he'd made a mistake in slipping her into handcuffs.

But damned if he'd let himself fall prey to her for a third time.

And the baby… He couldn't even think about that right now.

She had to be playing him. Had to be conspiring with the Watcher. There were no tracking devices anywhere on either of them. He had meticulously searched her clothes, his, her notebook and wallet and found nothing.

He'd watched mile after mile in the rearview mirror to make sure they weren't being followed. There was no way any one vehicle—hell, even two or three taking turns—could've followed without his knowing. Steve had been watching. No one had tailed them.

The only suspicious happening since they'd left Pensacola had been Rosalyn's call to the Ammonses. To a couple she'd previously stated had no phone in their house.

How exactly did you call someone who didn't have a phone?

You didn't.

But you could be calling a partner you were working with. Tip him off about where you were going. She might not have been able to give her partner specifics, but she could get him close enough that he could start tailing without Steve's awareness.

He remembered her head against the telephone cradle at lunch today. The same guilty expression she'd had while standing over at the car while he'd been talking to the local cops.

Like she felt bad for tipping her partner off, then felt bad again that Steve had been hurt.

He should be thankful for her guilty conscience. Without it, he would be dead.

Or maybe—if he was willing to give Rosalyn a slight benefit of the doubt—*maybe* she hadn't known exactly what her partner's plan was. Maybe she hadn't known the plan was to kill Steve outright.

Maybe she was a thief and a con but not a murderer.

The thought made him feel slightly better, which made him even angrier, which made his arm hurt like a bitch. Steve gritted his teeth. He'd have to take some aspirin when he got to Omega HQ, because he wasn't going anywhere else but there.

Not giving Rosalyn any chance to escape. He could've sworn she was about to run while he was talking to the cops. Maybe she'd known he was onto her.

He was surprised she didn't try to plead her case while it was just the two of them in the car. She had to know that once other people were involved—people not so blinded by their obvious gullibility for her like Steve—it would be harder for her to fool them. To fool him.

But she hadn't said anything. Not a single word since he'd put the cuffs on her. Hadn't gotten angry. Hadn't cried. Hadn't reasoned with him.

If he hadn't known better, he would've said she'd just shut down. Even now, she had her arms wrapped protectively around herself, around the baby. She was looking straight ahead, but it didn't seem like she saw anything.

Obviously she hadn't thought he would figure it out. At least not this soon.

There was only one thing Steve knew for absolute certain. He was going to get some answers. Maybe he couldn't trust his own judgment around Rosalyn. Was too close to her.

But he was taking her to Omega's Critical Response Division. He had some of the best profilers and behavioral analysts in the entire world working on his team. He might not be able to get to the truth with Rosalyn.

But they would.

STEVE SAW ROSALYN perk up a little when he pulled into the Omega complex. Obviously she hadn't been expecting him to take her somewhere as sophisticated as his unit.

That's right, sweetheart—you didn't just pick some local yokel to mess with. You're in the big leagues now.

"Not what you were expecting?"

She looked over at him. "I don't know what you think I was expecting, but no, this wasn't it." She turned back to look out the window. Her hands were rubbing at the handcuffs on her wrist.

He wondered if she wished she'd chosen her mark better. Or maybe getting some sort of information about Omega had been her plan all along.

He steeled himself against any softness toward her. He couldn't allow her to get the upper hand again. The cuffs were probably overkill, but it was a necessary reminder—for both of them—that she was a criminal.

When Steve walked in through the front door with Rosalyn, the guards did a double take. They were probably equally as disconcerted to see Steve in a casual shirt and jeans as they were to see him bringing in a prisoner. Neither were commonplace for Steve.

He went through standard procedures to enter the building, ID scan, weapon check-in. He signed in Rosalyn as being in his custody and walked her through the metal detector. She set it off, of course, because of the handcuffs.

The guard looked uncomfortable. "Um, protocol says we scan all prisoners entering the building, Mr. Drackett."

"That's fine." Steve didn't really like it, but damned if he'd give her preferential treatment.

Rosalyn raised her cuffed hands in front of her face so the guard could use the wand to run up the front of her body, then down the back. Nothing else set off the detector.

Steve had to admit he was a little relieved. If she'd had a hidden cell phone or weapon on her, he would've never been able to trust his own judgment again.

The guard allowed them through and he took Rosalyn's arm to the elevator and into the division offices.

As soon as he walked into the large open area that housed most of the desks of the Critical Response Division, Steve knew he had made a mistake. He should not have paraded Rosalyn in like this. He should've let the locals handle her arrest. There were going to be too many people with too many questions about who Rosalyn was and what was going on.

Personal questions.

Steve wanted answers from Rosalyn. But at the same time he did not want his private life being broadcast all over the office.

He looked over at her. Her head was bowed and her hair was framing her face on either side. Between her hunched shoulders, pregnant belly and handcuffs, she made quite the pitiful picture.

Steve wasn't surprised when Andrea Gordon, one of the most naturally gifted behavioral analysts Steve had ever known, approached them, her concerned look focused on Rosalyn.

Hell, even Steve felt sorry for her and she'd almost gotten him killed an hour ago.

"Steve, is there anything I can help with?" Andrea asked him.

"In a minute, Andrea." Steve glanced around until he found the person he wanted. He wasn't surprised to see him leaning against the wall on the other side of the room watching what was going on.

"Waterman!" Steve jerked his head to the side, indicating Derek should come over.

Derek Waterman, head of the Omega SWAT team, was always aware of what was going on around him. He was focused and deadly and an asset to the team for multiple reasons.

But right now Steve wanted Derek because of what he wasn't: friendly. Steve needed Rosalyn escorted down to an interrogation room. Most of the other men on the team would be friendly, try to set Rosalyn at ease. That's not what Steve wanted. He wanted Rosalyn nervous, uncomfortable, unhappy.

That's how he would get answers.

And if a little voice said he was making a huge mistake, well, he'd just squash that. He was done giving her the benefit of the doubt.

"Derek, will you please escort Ms. Mellinger to interview room 2?" It was the starkest of the interrogation rooms, the least comfortable.

Out of the corner of his eye he saw Andrea stiffen. She didn't like how he was treating Rosalyn. But then again, Andrea tended to be tenderhearted toward everyone.

Derek didn't even bat an eye. "No problem, boss." He turned to Rosalyn. "If you could come with me, ma'am." Respectful yet distant. He took her arm and escorted her down the hall.

Steve turned back from them and found at least a dozen of his team watching him.

"All right, people, let's get back to work. I know you have other things to do besides gape at me."

Many of them sat back down at their desks or went back to their normal tasks. Liam Goetz, hostage rescue team captain and resident smart-ass, just walked closer.

"But, boss, how are we supposed to go back to work when we know there's such a big, bad criminal nearby?"

That got a couple of snickers. Steve turned to Liam. "I can fire you, you know."

"If I had a dollar for every time you said that," Liam muttered, but eased back down to his desk.

The good thing about his team was that the members knew each other well enough to know when to leave something alone. He also knew he could trust them to provide him with the information he didn't seem capable of getting himself. Or have the neutrality required to do it.

"Brandon, Andrea, Jon, I need to see you in my office."

He turned and walked out of the main room. He didn't check to see if the people he'd asked for were following. He knew they were. If for curiosity's sake as much as anything else.

He walked through his outer office door. Cynthia and his other assistants stood when they saw him, all with pressing matters that needed his attention, he was sure. He held out a hand.

"For the next few hours, unless there is a national

or international crisis, consider me still unavailable. I don't want to know about it." He saw Brandon and Andrea make eye contact with each other at his words but didn't care. For his own sanity, unless there was some sort of real emergency, he had to get this issue with Rosalyn settled.

"Do you need something for your arm?" Andrea asked. All eyes flew to it. Damn it, he'd been trying not to let anyone know about the throb and what he was sure was going to be stiff and painful tomorrow. He glared at Andrea for bringing it up. He should've known she'd be able to read his nonverbal communication too accurately for him to hide or fake.

"Sorry." She shrugged. "It wasn't that noticeable, but I could tell."

"What happened?" Brandon asked.

"I was on the wrong side of a steel telescopic baton." Steve grimaced. "I'm fine."

"I'll get ice and ibuprofen. It will help with swelling and pain. We'll handle everything, Steve." Cynthia, the assistant who'd been with the team the longest, the one he trusted the most, nodded at him. "You handle your crisis. We'll handle anything else."

Steve opened the door for his inner office and held it for the others. Jon Hatton and Brandon Han were two of the finest profilers—honestly two of the most brilliant, trustworthy men—Steve had ever known. Andrea was much quieter and kept to herself more due to her past, but as a behavioral analyst she couldn't be beat.

"What's going on, Steve?" Jon asked. "I'm assuming that woman you walked in with was the Rosalyn Mellinger you had me looking into."

Steve went over to the window looking out at the Rockies. Normally the view gave him a measure of peace, but not right now. "She is."

"You didn't mention she was having a baby."

"No." Steve shook his head. He really didn't want to get into that yet if he didn't have to. "I didn't."

"You also didn't mention that she was a suspect." He could hear the frustration in Jon's voice. "That would've changed how I was reading the information."

Steve turned and looked at them. "She wasn't a suspect until lunchtime and then about an hour ago."

He explained what had happened with the phone call and the attack at the gas station. He was just finishing as Margaret, another one of his assistants, brought in the pain medication and some ice. Someone had also dug up a sling. That would at least take the pressure off his shoulder and hopefully ease some of the throbbing. He thanked her.

"What did Rosalyn say to your accusations?" Brandon asked as Steve took the medication.

"She denied them, of course."

Andrea walked over and helped him ease his arm into the sling. Immediately the pain eased somewhat.

"And you're not completely sure about your accusations either," she said softly. "You're angry with her, but also protective. And confused most of all."

Steve nodded. "Yes. All of those things." He looked over at the other two men. "I've lost my perspective when it comes to Rosalyn Mellinger."

"Because the baby is yours," Brandon said. Jon nodded, not looking surprised.

Steve shrugged. "She says so."

Andrea touched his arm. "It's okay to believe her. Until you know for sure otherwise, it's okay to believe that what she says about that is true."

"Well, if it is, then it seems an awful lot like she was just part of a plan to kill or at least seriously injure the father of her baby."

He walked around his desk and looked out at the three of them. "I can't be neutral around her. So I need you three to figure out the truth for me. To be my eyes and ears."

Chapter Fifteen

Rosalyn sat in a room that was like something out of a crime-investigation show on television. A table with four chairs around it, none of them comfortable, cement walls all the way around painted a gray color that wasn't very different from their original hue. Fluorescent lights blared down from overhead, unflattering at best, downright painful after a few hours.

And on one wall was a large mirror covering half the surface. Of course, it would be a two-way mirror.

She'd known Steve was in law enforcement, but she'd had no idea he worked at a place like this. That he was evidently the *boss* in a place like this.

She'd told him everything she knew about the Watcher and he'd just made it seem like he was a beat cop or something. He was obviously so much more than that. He hadn't tried to give her any insight or any knowledge about what he thought would be the next steps.

Because he hadn't trusted her. She could almost understand the misunderstanding with the phone and the guy on the motorcycle. But Steve hadn't trusted her from the beginning. Not today, not last night when they were making love, not ever.

She'd started feeling like she was finally not alone, not knowing she was actually more alone than ever.

The guy who had brought her down to this stark room hadn't been mean or rough. He hadn't said much to her at all, beyond reading her the Miranda rights. Rosalyn wondered if she should call a lawyer but didn't know one to call here. Plus, she hadn't done anything wrong.

Besides trust that Steve Drackett was looking out for her best interests.

The big guy—what had Steve called him? Derek?—had escorted her to her seat.

"Stay here," had been all she'd gotten out of him before he'd left, closing the door behind him with a resounding click.

How long ago had that been? Probably twenty minutes. It felt like hours. Rosalyn could feel panic scratching at her subconscious, trying to work its way in. She refused to let it. She hadn't done anything wrong. Surely someone would believe her.

Although she was quite sure it wouldn't be Steve.

And once someone did believe her and she got out of here, where was she going to go? The Watcher had found her again. She wrapped her still-handcuffed arms around her belly, rocking back and forth, fighting panic once again.

What was she going to do?

Rosalyn nearly jumped out of her seat as the door opened. Two men, both of whom had been out in the office when Steve had brought her in, entered.

"Are you okay, Ms. Mellinger?" One, a stunningly handsome Asian man, asked her. He looked genuinely concerned.

"I just…I just…" The words wouldn't come out.

I just realized the enormity of the fact that a killer has found me again and the one person I thought I could trust wants to throw me in jail.

"I was just startled. That's all," she finally finished.

They both came and sat in the chairs on the other side of the table. The other man, very tall and also handsome, had a key in his hands. "Can I take those handcuffs off? I'm sure you'll be more comfortable without them."

Rosalyn brought her wrists up to the table so he could release her. She had to get some measure of control over herself. She could do this.

"Are you sure you fellas will feel safe with me unfettered?" She raised an eyebrow at them. They both had her by nearly a foot and at least fifty pounds apiece. Not to mention her range of motion with her extended belly would make her escape skills almost nonexistent.

Both men glanced at each other and cracked a smile. "We'll be sure to keep our guard up," the tall one said. "I'm Jon Hatton and this is Brandon Han. We're both profilers and behavioral analysts here at the Critical Response Division of Omega Sector."

"I'm not sure I know exactly what Omega Sector is."

Agent Han leaned back in his chair. "We're an interagency task force. People working together with backgrounds in the FBI, DEA, ATF and other relevant agencies. We even have some Interpol and other international agencies as part of our ranks. Helps us cut through red tape."

"We'd like to ask you some questions about what happened at the gas station a couple of hours ago," Hatton said. "Did you know the man on the motorcycle was going to attack Steve?"

"No." She looked at one man and then the other. "I was inside the store when I saw the guy pull up. I thought it was pretty stupid that he was coming right behind our car when there were other pumps open, but I didn't know who he was or that he was going to hurt Steve until I saw him flick out his stick thing."

Agent Han had pulled out a notebook and began writing. "It's called a telescopic baton. A weapon that can be easily transported and then, like you said, be fully expanded with just a flick of the wrist."

She nodded. "Steve was looking at me, so I knew he wasn't paying attention to the guy and was going to get hurt." She remembered knowing she wouldn't get outside in time to warn him. "Fortunately, Steve turned at the last second and blocked the hit with his arm."

"And you had no idea who the man was or that he was going to be there at that time?" Han asked.

"No." Rosalyn could feel the panic pulling at her again.

Hatton tilted his head to the side. "You didn't notify him in any way that you were traveling to Colorado Springs with Steve?"

It was almost like it was a friendly question. That this was all some dinner-party conversation. Rosalyn could feel hysteria building up inside her and fought to keep it tamped down.

"No. I did not contact the man who has been stalking me almost daily for the last year, who has caused me to leave my job, all my friends, and for six months live on the run in sleazy hotels. I did not contact the man who has driven me to the precipice of insanity and thoughts of suicide more than once."

She leaned forward in her chair. "I did not contact the man from whom I, for the first time in a year, had found a measure of peace because I had finally felt like I had gotten away from him for good. I did not bring that man back into my life."

Agent Han leaned forward too. "Then how did he find you and Steve?"

Rosalyn couldn't stop the tears now. "I don't know," she whispered before huddling back into her chair. "He always finds me."

The two men looked at her for a long time. Rosalyn finally just covered her face with her hands.

After a long pause she heard Agent Hatton say, "I think we need to start at the beginning."

STEVE WATCHED IT all from the adjacent room, able to see everything through the two-way mirror and hear everything through the audio that was pumped in. Andrea had wanted to go in with Brandon to help question Rosalyn, but Steve had asked her to stay.

He needed Andrea's opinion. Not only could she read other people's nonverbal communication with remarkable accuracy, she also had a sixth sense about their emotions. She could feel what they were emoting even if it didn't match what the person was saying.

He'd trusted Andrea's abilities when he'd pulled her

out of a pretty horrible situation nearly five years ago; he trusted them even more now.

"Steve, I've got to say, there is nothing Rosalyn has done nonverbally that has given me any indication that she's not telling the truth."

Rosalyn had started back at the beginning like Jon had asked her to do. She'd spent the last hour telling Jon and Brandon about the Watcher and everything that had happened. She was giving much more detail than she had to him.

It made him physically ill to think about what she'd gone through.

Steve rubbed his good hand over his face, his hurt arm still in the sling. He didn't have to have Andrea's talent at reading people to see that Rosalyn was telling the truth.

"I've made a pretty bad mistake."

Andrea looked at him, eyebrow raised.

"When the attacker showed up at the gas station, just a couple of hours after she'd made what I deemed to be a suspicious phone call, I was positive she'd played me again."

"Again?"

Steve realized this all came back to when Rosalyn had left him at the hotel six months ago without a word.

"She fooled me. Snuck out in the middle of the night. Took all my cash."

Andrea studied him. Steve knew he wouldn't like whatever it was she was going to say.

"She hurt you."

"My pride, sure. Personally and professionally. I'm the head of one of the most prestigious law enforcement agencies in the world. If I can't tell when I'm being set up as a mark, maybe I don't deserve to run this place."

Andrea shook her head, the tiniest of smiles on her face. "No, it's a lot more than that. You opened yourself to her and she hurt you."

Steve thought of that time in Pensacola before Rosalyn had fled. He had known she was scared of something, that something was happening in her life. He'd planned to ask her to stay with him the rest of the week. Hell, if being outside made her nervous for whatever reason, they could stay in the bungalow.

He'd planned to keep her there, to make love to her, to talk to her and listen to her until she realized she could trust him. Then they could solve whatever scared her together. Maybe he'd even see if she needed a fresh start in Colorado. She'd mentioned the beautiful mountains.

Steve ran his hand through his hair. He couldn't deny it to himself any longer. He, jaded law enforcement officer who saw the worst of humanity on a daily basis, who hadn't been on more than a handful of dates since his wife died, had fallen in love at first sight. Or at the very least had been willing to try a relationship with Rosalyn, invite her into his life.

But she'd bailed before he had the chance.

So yeah, she had hurt him.

And evidently he still hadn't forgiven her for any of it. Because he'd put cuffs on her, for God's sake, and had her dragged into their least comfortable interrogation room like she was a terrorist or murderer or something.

"Damn it." He ran his hand over his face again. "I'm an idiot. I've got to get her out of there."

Andrea touched him on his arm. "Let Jon and Brandon finish talking to her. It's helping her, Steve. To go through the details. To talk about it with someone else."

Steve watched through the mirror again and saw Andrea was right, as she most always was. Rosalyn was sitting up straight, had unwrapped her arms from the protective stance around herself. Her shoulders weren't hunched. She had more color in her cheeks.

Brandon had asked for Rosalyn's notebook when she'd mentioned it, and it had been brought to them. The three of them were now poring over it.

Obviously Jon and Brandon believed Rosalyn, and were trying to help her make sense of it all. To discover the pattern in the Watcher's actions concerning her.

Exactly what Steve should've been doing rather than worrying about whether she was in on her own terrorizing.

Derek Waterman entered the room. "Some more info for you, boss, about the Ammonses in Georgia. Seems like they don't have a phone in their house, but they do have one at their café, for orders and such."

Of course they did.

"We checked, and there was a record of a call from Dalhart, Texas, made to them this morning at ten o'clock Eastern time. I think that would line up with the call Rosalyn was making."

"Yep, it definitely would. Thanks, Derek."

And just like that, Rosalyn was cleared. Although he'd already cleared her in his mind anyway.

Derek turned toward the mirror. "She looks a lot better than she did when I brought her in there."

"That's because the idiot quota surrounding her has dropped significantly." Steve grimaced.

Derek chuckled. "Hey, only my wife is allowed to call me an idiot."

"Your wife is a certified genius. She's at liberty to call everyone an idiot." Derek's wife, Molly, was the head of the Omega forensic lab. "But in this case, I was referring to myself."

Derek slapped him on the shoulder and Steve winced from the blow he'd taken there but didn't say anything. "We all can be idiots when it comes to the women we care about."

Steve heard a muttered "Amen" out of Andrea.

"Andrea, will you take some food and water in to them? Make sure Rosalyn is okay? I don't want to disrupt their progress by going in there myself."

"Sure. That's a good idea. I'm sure she'll appreciate your thoughtfulness, Steve."

He shook his head. "No, don't say it's from me. Just make sure she has what she needs."

Steve wasn't sure Rosalyn was ever going to want to talk to him again after how he'd treated her. All he could do now was catch the psycho trying to harm them both.

Steve would do whatever it took to keep Rosalyn and their baby safe. And would pray she would give him another chance.

Chapter Sixteen

They believed her. She wasn't exactly sure when it happened, but Rosalyn knew Agents Hatton and Han believed her.

The gorgeous blonde who'd first approached her in the offices before Steve stopped her came into the room. She had a tray of food—some soup and crackers—and water and coffee.

"We thought you might want something to eat. And Steve mentioned you like coffee."

"Steve sent you in here with food and drink? I thought he wanted me thrown under the jail."

The woman set the tray down in front of Rosalyn, then went to stand beside Brandon's chair. He hooked a casual arm around her hips. What a striking couple those two made.

She smiled gently at Rosalyn. "Sometimes it's difficult to see things that are right in front of you when there are feelings involved. I'm sure that's true for Steve."

"I think Steve made it quite obvious he has no feelings for me when he arrested me a few hours ago."

The woman smiled. "Sometimes men are a little bit

slower in recognizing their own feelings." The woman looked over at Brandon and a moment of tenderness passed between them. Obviously at some point Brandon had been a little slow in recognizing his feelings for the woman. Although obviously not anymore.

"I'm Andrea Gordon, by the way." Andrea looked back up at Rosalyn. "And just for the record, you are not under arrest. You're free to leave at any time, although we would very much like you to stay so we can continue working on the case with you."

"Does Steve Drackett know I'm free to go?"

Andrea nodded. "He's the one who gave the word."

Rosalyn didn't know what to make of that, so she just started eating her food.

The other three agents began looking at the papers on the table.

"Steve found two transmitters on Rosalyn's personal effects. One was on a sweater, one on her bag," Jon said and turned his attention to her. "He found those after the fire at the hotel, right?"

Rosalyn nodded. "While we were at the hospital, I think."

"And you went immediately to the superstore and changed out of everything?"

"Yes, the only thing I took with me out of that store that I had brought in was this notebook." She pointed at the one on the table.

Jon looked through it. "It's highly unlikely that there's any sort of transmitter in here, but let's get it scanned just in case." He walked out of the room with it.

Brandon sat back in his chair, taking a cracker Rosalyn offered him from her tray. "Let's say he got the transmitters on you at the very beginning. That he broke into your house and put one on every piece of clothing you had. That would be excessive and expensive, but this is obviously no garden-variety stalker we're dealing with here."

"That's how he followed you for the first six months. He knew where you were and could show up there," Andrea continued.

Jon walked back into the room. "Derek's going to take the notebook over to Molly in the lab."

"We're trying to figure out the transmitter pattern," Brandon told him. "I'm running with the possibility that he put trackers on everything she owned at the beginning."

"Okay," Jon said. "Possible. And scary."

Rosalyn had to agree.

Brandon continued. "When we get your notebook back, we'll double-check for patterns to see if there's any consistency, but maybe he was working around his own schedule. He has a job that requires him to be in an office at least part of the time. That's why some weeks you had notes multiple days in a row, and sometimes you didn't hear from him for a while."

Jon nodded. "That would suggest someone with a career. We can see if weekends were more active with the notes—that might help confirm."

Rosalyn looked at them. "I don't understand. You're saying the Watcher is just a normal guy? Like a businessman or a lawyer or something?" The thought made her feel a little ill.

Andrea reached over and touched her hand. "A lot

of times minds of pure evil can be dressed in very professional packages."

Brandon shrugged. "Times you thought he was toying with you by leaving you alone, making you think you'd gotten away? Maybe he just had something in his schedule that required his attention and he couldn't get to you that day."

"And it is highly likely that the Watcher is from your hometown of Mobile, since that's where it all started. Not only that, but that you know him or met him briefly." Jon grimaced.

Rosalyn shuddered, glad she was almost done with her food. She wouldn't have been able to eat another bite after thinking about this. "I was an accountant. I met with clients all the time."

"We'll check into that right away," Jon said. "Clients you've met with, coworkers."

"But really, it could be anyone. Someone I met at the grocery store or while waiting for the elevator."

Rosalyn saw the compassion in Andrea's eyes. "Yes, unfortunately."

The thought that she might recognize the Watcher's face when they caught him made her want to be physically ill. Every person she'd known was suspect.

But for the first time, Rosalyn actually had hope that they—this Omega Sector team—might really catch him. Before today her only hope had been she might be able to outrun him at some point. Get somewhere he couldn't find her. But there hadn't been much chance of that with the baby coming.

Jon, Brandon and Andrea were discussing particular aspects of the Watcher when the door to the room opened and Steve walked in.

They just stared at each other for a long time. Apology was clear all over his face.

But even with his arm in the sling and the stiffness in his frame—pain from being hit with that telescopic baton thing—Rosalyn found she wasn't quite ready to let this go just yet.

Steve eventually stepped away from the door.

"All right, I've cleared conference room 1 for us to use. I think we'll all be more comfortable there."

Everybody stood and began packing up their notes, still talking about the Watcher they were trying to profile.

"Rosalyn and I will meet you up there in a few minutes."

They all shuffled out quickly after that. Rosalyn remained in her chair. Steve came and sat across from her.

"I overreacted. Made a mistake."

She cocked her head to the side. "You thought I tried to have you killed."

"You made a suspicious phone call and a few hours later someone took a swing at my head with a metal rod. That seemed pretty dubious at the time."

"I told you I called the Ammonses." Her volume began to rise.

His did too. "You also told me the day before that the Ammonses didn't have a phone. It seemed like an inconsistency in your story. You know who tends to have inconsistencies in their stories? Liars and criminals."

Rosalyn rolled her eyes. "I called their café. They have a phone there."

His eyes narrowed. "I know that *now*. But you didn't tell me that."

Rosalyn stood, bracing her hands on the table and leaning toward him. "Because you didn't ask. Because you were convinced I was up to no good. That I was playing you."

"Damn it, Rosalyn, I'm trained to look for suspicious patterns. To see bad things before they happen."

"And that's what I was, right? A bad thing."

"No, it's just—"

She slammed her hand down on the table. "You put handcuffs on me like I was some common criminal that might try to run at any second. You didn't ask. You didn't give me a chance to explain."

"Rosalyn—"

"We made love last night. And today you were convinced I was trying to have you killed. I guess that tells me how you really feel about me."

He stood then. "No, it wasn't like that. I had to force myself to try to look at you objectively."

He reached out toward her, but she snatched herself back. When Steve touched her, she couldn't think straight. Her attraction to him overpowered everything else. She didn't want that now. Maybe never wanted it again.

She rubbed her eyes. She was tired, not just from today but from everything. The only thing good going for her now was the fact that everyone here believed her. The agents seemed ready and willing to put their resources and brainpower into figuring out who the

Watcher was and what Rosalyn could do about it. It was more than she'd had in a long time.

"You know what? Just take me to the conference room. The faster we can get this situation resolved, the sooner I can get myself out of your life."

Because Steve obviously didn't want her there.

STEVE DIDN'T MAKE a lot of tactical errors. Nor did he make many errors in judgment. His job and the lives of the people on his team, not to mention those of the American public in general, depended on it.

But he'd done both with Rosalyn.

They walked to the conference room together in silence. Not the comfortable kind.

She was mad. He didn't blame her.

But she was right. They needed to concentrate on figuring out all they could about the Watcher. Not because Steve wanted Rosalyn out of his life—he'd be damned if he was going to let that happen—but because obviously the Watcher had escalated in violence over the past few days.

Steve would do whatever was necessary to keep Rosalyn and the baby safe. Even if she didn't want anything to do with him right now.

He held the door open for her as they entered the conference room. Jon, Brandon and Andrea were already there. Roman Weber, a member of Omega's SWAT team, had joined them.

One entire wall of the conference room was made up of an electronic whiteboard. Brandon and Jon had already started making a timeline on it. Everything they wrote could be saved onto a computer file to be used later.

"Molly brought Rosalyn's notebook back over from the lab," Andrea said as they walked in. "Nothing suspicious about it."

Steve nodded, not surprised.

Brandon turned to them from the whiteboard. "Basically, we have two inconsistencies that need to be addressed before we can go much further. First, why didn't the Watcher have any contact with you for the six months you were at the Ammonses' in Ellijay? What was different? Something in your life or something in his?"

"I don't know." Rosalyn shrugged as she sat down at the table.

"How did you meet them?" Andrea asked.

"I took a bus from Pensacola as far as the amount of money I had would take me." She glanced over at Steve, then looked away quickly. "That ended up being Ellijay.

"The Ammonses own a small café in town. They've lived there all their lives. They live right on top of the café, although I know Mr. Ammons also has a fishing cabin somewhere." Rosalyn smiled. "I got off the bus, went in to eat and felt like I never really left there again until I went to meet my sister in Pensacola."

Her smile faded into a flinch at the mention of her sister.

"Anyway, I asked Mrs. Ammons if I could make some cash washing dishes or whatever. They're not big fans of the government, so they didn't mind paying me cash under the table."

Jon smiled. "I like them already."

She shrugged, shaking her head with a smile. "The Ammonses are odd. Definitely keep to themselves and don't want people, especially the government, in their business. But they took me in. Let me wash dishes, then started letting me wait tables. When they found out I was sleeping out back under the café's overhang—"

"What?" The word was out of Steve's mouth before he could catch it. But the thought of her homeless, pregnant, sleeping outside.

"Honestly, it wasn't so bad. And it was just for a few days."

Steve's fist clenched but he didn't say anything further.

"Anyway, they invited me to live with them, and that was that. I pretty much never left their property. I worked, then went upstairs. For the first couple of weeks I would run downstairs every morning to see if there was a note from the Watcher."

"And nothing? Ever?" Brandon asked.

"No. Never. I just began thinking of the house as my force field." She scoffed at herself. "Stupid, I know."

Andrea walked over and touched Rosalyn on the shoulder. "No, not stupid at all. No one would blame you for staying somewhere where you felt safe. Where, for all intents and purposes, you *were* safe."

"Why did you leave?" Jon asked.

"The baby." Rosalyn put a hand on her stomach. "Soon it wasn't just going to be me anymore. The Ammonses are in their seventies. I knew I needed to have a backup plan in case..." She trailed off, then finally picked back up. "In case something happened to me."

In case the Watcher killed her. She didn't say it but everyone in the room knew what she meant.

"So you contacted your sister," Andrea prompted when Rosalyn didn't go on.

She nodded. "I asked Lindsey to meet me in Pensacola. I was going to go back to the hotel and see if they would give me Steve's name. Or, if there was some sort of privacy law, see if they would at least contact him on my behalf."

Until that moment Steve hadn't realized he'd held a hardness inside himself against her about that. He'd silently, subconsciously, assumed she'd never planned to tell him about the baby. But she had. He took a step toward her, catching her eyes with his.

"I didn't know who you were," she continued, looking at him. "And I definitely didn't know about all this—" she gestured around the room with her arm "—but I knew the baby had a better chance with you than with me."

He wanted to move closer. To pick her up and plop her down on his lap. To promise her it was all going to be all right. To apologize for being an idiot earlier today.

Andrea looked over at him, sympathy in her eyes. She could clearly read his pain, his concern. Steve didn't care if it was noticeable to everyone.

"And Steve was there identifying what he thought was your body," Jon said.

"With all your sister's drug troubles, I'm surprised her prints weren't on file. But yours were," Steve said. "At least from juvie."

Rosalyn rolled her eyes. "That's when we were six-teen and Lindsey shoplifted. Left me to take the blame."

It explained a lot.

"Okay." Brandon got them back on track. "And once you were in Pensacola, you were immediately con-tacted by the Watcher again."

Rosalyn's lips pursed as she nodded.

"We know your clothes had the transmitters. Maybe they were short-range and the Watcher couldn't pick them up from that far away," Jon mused.

"Possible, but Rosalyn also traveled nearly as far when she was in Dallas and Memphis and he found her there." Brandon turned back toward the whiteboard.

It was time to take action. Steve turned to Roman. "I need you to get to Ellijay. Talk to the Ammonses, scope out the situation. See why the Watcher might have left Rosalyn alone while she was there."

Roman headed for the door. "You got it, boss. One-horse towns are my favorite." He winked at everyone as he walked by. "I'll call as soon as I have info."

Brandon nodded. "Good. Having solid intel on the Ammonses will help. The other big inconsistency is how the Watcher found you here in Colorado, after you'd removed all the bugs."

Steve ran a hand over his face. "I could've sworn we weren't followed. I was actively watching the en-tire time." He looked over at Rosalyn and shrugged. "But today hasn't been my finest day when it comes to judgment calls."

Jon had been looking at Rosalyn's notebook but now

looked up to address everyone. "I think we all have to agree. We're either missing something big, or the Watcher isn't just one person."

Chapter Seventeen

The thought that she had one psychopathic stalker had been bad enough. Jon Hatton's idea that it might actually be more than one person had been enough to put Rosalyn into a panic.

She hadn't said anything, had just tried to keep it all together while all the discussion continued on around her. They'd sent someone out for pizza, and Rosalyn had done her best to eat, but it had been difficult.

Eventually she'd put a hand on Steve's arm. Once he'd gotten a good look at her, he'd immediately announced he was taking her home.

His home.

He called Derek Waterman and another SWAT member she hadn't met yet named Liam Goetz. They were tasked with making sure no one followed them to Steve's house. Liam joked and flirted with her, when he wasn't showing her pictures of his newborn twins, while Steve personally inspected the Omega vehicle they'd be using. Evidently it had already been swept thoroughly for bugs, but he wanted to double-check.

They drove around for more than an hour. Derek went to Steve's house and checked it out for them.

They even switched vehicles halfway through their journey. There was no way anyone could've followed them. Hell, Rosalyn was in the car and she hardly knew where they were.

"I couldn't find my way back to your building now if my life depended on it." She had long since closed her eyes, but having them open wouldn't have helped anyway.

"Believe it or not, my house is only a few miles away from the office. We're just taking the scenic route."

"I don't think anyone could've followed us."

Steve grimaced. "I thought the same was true earlier today, but I was wrong. But both Derek and Liam have given us the all clear. So I'm certain no one has followed us now. Plus, we'll have a guard in a car outside the house watching for anyone."

"Derek?"

"No, someone else. Derek will want to get home to his wife and their daughter."

"Yeah, Liam was showing me pictures of his twins and his daughter, Tallinn."

Steve smiled. "Yes, he and his wife, Vanessa, adopted her after a human-trafficking case last year. And the twins...they're just exhausting. Keeps Vanessa and Liam busy."

Rosalyn realized how little she knew about the man she was about to have a baby with. She opened her eyes. "How about you? Do you have any kids? You were married once right?"

"Yes. Melanie. She died in a car accident twelve years ago. But no, we didn't have any kids."

"I'm sorry about your wife." Rosalyn wondered if Steve still loved her.

"Don't take this the wrong way, but you two would've liked each other. Both of you are smart and strong." His smile was pensive, but not sad.

"Do you still love her?" The words were out before she could bite off her tongue. Damn it. "Never mind. You don't have to answer that."

"No, it's okay. I'll always love Melanie—she was a huge part of my life." He looked over at her before returning his gaze to the road. "But no, I'm not in love with her anymore. Not pining after her. As a matter of fact, she'd probably lay into me for taking this long to get serious about someone."

Was that what they were? Serious?

"Do you mean us?"

"You're the only person I'm having a baby with."

"You arrested me earlier today, for heaven's sake."

He grimaced. "I was trying to do the right thing. To keep some perspective. My perspective has been blown to hell since the day you ran into that bar in Pensacola trying to get out of the rain."

"Because I stole from you?"

"No. I couldn't care less about the money. Because you got under my skin the way no one else has."

He pulled the car into a driveway of a small house, then used his phone to activate a code that opened the garage door.

She turned to look at him more fully.

"I did?" She had figured he'd be a little irritated at her running off with his cash, then would never think about her again.

He pressed the button to shut the garage door and turned off the car but still stared straight ahead with his hand on the wheel. "Why do you think I happened to be in Pensacola to identify your body? I had the Pensacola police report sent to my desk every day."

"To look for me? Because you thought I would be arrested?"

"I figured if you were looking for businessmen as marks to steal from, you would eventually get caught."

After her behavior in Florida, she really couldn't blame him for that conclusion, although it still sat heavy in her heart. "And you wanted to press charges too."

"That's what I told myself." He finally looked at her. "But really it was so I could find you again, rescue you from the terrible path I thought you were walking down and bring you back here. Set you straight."

"You sound like a parole officer."

He continued as if she hadn't spoken, his eyes softening. "And then once you were more settled, with a good job and happy with your life, I planned to court you properly. To go out on dates and get to know you."

"Oh."

"Because there has not been one single day that I haven't thought of you. I'll admit, I wasn't always happy with you. But I also have to admit that my plan, once I found you again, was to make sure we were together. Even when I thought you were a petty criminal."

"But you don't think I'm one anymore?"

He reached over and tucked a strand of hair behind her ear. "No."

She asked the question she'd been afraid to ask. "And you believe me when I say the baby is yours?"

"Yes." His hand slid into her hair and pulled her closer. "And I'm going to do whatever it takes to keep you and the baby safe."

He closed the distance between their lips. Soft, this time, full of promise but not demand. His thumb brushed along her jaw, sending a rush of sensation racing across her skin. She leaned in closer but stopped when she felt the oddest sensation in her belly.

She jumped back from Steve. "Whoa." She put both hands on her stomach.

"What? Are you okay? Is something wrong?"

She smiled. "I'm fine. He just kicked. Like, kicked *really* hard."

She grabbed his hand not in the sling and put it on her stomach under her hand. They waited a moment, and then she felt it again.

Steve's eyes grew wide. "I felt that."

Rosalyn's smile felt so big that it might split her face. "I know! He must be a soccer player or something."

"Have you felt him move before?"

"I think so, but I thought it was indigestion or something. Never anything this strong."

They waited a few minutes more, but evidently their little soccer player had gotten tired. Both Rosalyn and Steve were still grinning as he helped her out of the car and led her into the house.

In the midst of all the heartbreak and chaos of the last two days, feeling their baby move so lively inside her made everything seem like it was going to be okay.

But that didn't stop her from being tired. Steve

showed her around as they talked. He stopped and turned to her when they got to the kitchen.

"I don't have much food." He grimaced. "Honestly, I don't usually come here very often during the week. There's a small apartment within the Omega complex I use. Or just crash on the couch in my office. But I could have an agent deliver us something."

"No, I'm fine tonight. Although I know I'll be hungry in the morning." She was always hungry first thing in the morning, but at least she didn't wake up sick anymore like she had in the first few months.

"I've got waffles and toaster pastries."

"Do the important people you work with know you eat Pop-Tarts for breakfast?"

He winked at her. "Please don't tell."

"Would it ruin your big, bad reputation?"

"No." He rolled his eyes. "They would all just want me to bring them some every day."

Rosalyn's laugh turned into a huge yawn.

Steve walked over and slid his good arm around her shoulder. "I guess that answers my question about whether you're ready for sleep or not."

He led her up the stairs to a bedroom. "This is my room. You can sleep here and I'll sleep in the guest room."

She grabbed his arm as he turned to go. "No, stay here with me."

"Rosalyn, are you sure? What I did today…" His head dropped.

"A little overdramatic to be sure, Director." She put a finger under his chin and lifted until they were looking at each other. "But the situation is complicated. If nothing else, I can definitely agree with that. So don't worry about it. We have a big enough enemy to fight without fighting each other."

"Then I would very much love to sleep in that bed with you, where I can hold you and know you and the baby are safe."

She pressed herself up against him and smiled. "Well, I hope not *just* hold…"

TRUE TO HIS WORD, Steve was still wrapped around Rosalyn when she woke up the next morning. Despite all her naughty intentions, she had fallen asleep not a minute after her head hit the pillow.

She eased herself away from Steve and out of the bed so she could use the bathroom and go make some breakfast. Actually, the infamous toaster pastries sounded just about perfect right now, although she still had to snicker a little bit.

She was dressed in one of Steve's T-shirts, a soft gray one that fell to her knees even over her extended belly. She never wanted to get out of it. But it would probably look a little weird if she wore it back to the Omega offices.

Rosalyn made her way down the stairs and into the kitchen, trying to rub sleep out of her eyes. She easily found the breakfast food in Steve's pantry—he hadn't been kidding when he said he didn't have much food here—and started decaf coffee. She ate the first Pop-Tart right out of the toaster to ease her growling stomach, then poured herself some coffee.

Hopefully they would make progress today. Real

progress. If anybody could, it was Steve's team. They were trained and obviously good at what they did.

She grabbed a plate of the breakfast food whose name was not to be spoken and another cup of coffee to take up to Steve. They'd have to leave soon, but maybe she could talk him into a little naughtiness before then.

She stepped out of the kitchen into the front hall and froze.

An envelope sat there on the ground, a garish white on Steve's dark hardwood floors. It had been slid under the front door at some point—she had no idea when. She could see her name on the front in bold letters.

Just like all the others she'd received over the past year.

The coffee cups slipped through her numb fingers and crashed to the floor, shattering. Rosalyn felt the drops of hot coffee burn her bare legs and feet almost from a distance.

She couldn't take her eyes off the envelope.

The Watcher had found her again.

Chapter Eighteen

Steve heard the shattering cups and jumped out of bed. He instantly realized Rosalyn wasn't in the room with him. Habit had him grabbing his sidearm before running toward the stairs.

"Rosalyn?"

He saw her standing there, perfectly still. Two cups lay broken at her feet.

"Are you okay? Don't move. You might cut yourself. What happened?"

Now that he knew she was safe, his adrenaline slowed just a little bit. He set his gun on the hallway table and walked toward her.

She'd dropped the coffee cups, but it didn't look like she was cut or burned.

"Are you all right?" he asked again. "I don't see any cuts."

When he looked up and saw her face, his concern came rushing back. She stood devoid of all color, fists pressed to the sides of her head. She was looking at him, trying to say something.

Glass be damned, he walked all the way to her.

"What, sweetheart? What's wrong? Is it the baby?"

He put his hand on her belly. She lowered her hands and he looked down to see her pointing to something on the floor.

"It's him," she whispered. "I know it's him. He found me."

It was a letter. Steve muttered the foulest expletive he knew. How the hell had the Watcher found them here? Ignoring the ache in his arm, Steve reached down and scooped Rosalyn up and carried her over to the stairs.

"Stay right here, okay?"

She nodded, but he wasn't sure she was processing anything he said. She just stared at the envelope on the ground, face ashen.

Steve got his weapon and did a sweep of the house to make sure no one had entered unawares, then called Derek.

"My house has been compromised," Steve said before Derek could even get a greeting in.

Derek's expletive matched Steve's.

"There's a letter here on my floor. Has been slid under the door. The house is secure now." Steve looked over to where Rosalyn sat huddled on the stairs, arms around her knees, rocking herself back and forth. "Who was on patrol last night?"

"Wilson. I'll call you back in two minutes." Derek disconnected the call.

Steve wanted to go over and open the letter. Read it. But more than that he wanted the forensics team to be able to get off any possible information. He walked over to stand by Rosalyn, rubbing her hair gently. He wished he could pick her up and carry her away but knew they had to deal with this while they could.

True to his word, Derek called back in a little over a minute. His voice was grim. "Wilson hasn't reported in for the last three hours and is not answering his phone now."

"Damn it." That was not a good sign.

"You should have agents at your door in three to four minutes. Liam is on his way, ETA ten minutes. I called Brandon and Andrea too. I figured Andrea might be good for Rosalyn."

"Thanks, Derek."

He could hear Derek's muted talking to someone before he came back on the line. "Molly and I are coming too. She wants to check out the scene herself. She says not to touch anything."

"Okay."

"Just hold tight, boss. We're on our way."

THIRTY MINUTES LATER his house was a circus.

He'd gotten Rosalyn back upstairs before anyone arrived. Helped her wash off the coffee that had spilled on her legs and they both got dressed.

She still hadn't said much. Still had no color in her face. But she was holding it together. That was all he could ask for.

Agent Wilson was dead. Had been shot at close range in his car. Initial estimates put his death at around 3:00 a.m.

Molly Humphries-Waterman and her forensic lab team were doing their job all over his front porch, Agent Wilson's car and around the letter itself.

When Brandon and Andrea got there, Steve sent her straight up to his room to where Rosalyn still sat on the bed.

The rest of his inner team—Derek, Jon, Liam and Brandon—were with Steve in the kitchen. Those were the men he trusted most in the world.

"We need to get Rosalyn moved to Omega," Jon said. "At least we know there that she'll be safe. That he can't get to her."

Brandon nodded. "I agree. There's something we missed, obviously. Some way he's finding Rosalyn's location."

"Because they sure as hell weren't followed." Liam leaned his large frame against the fridge. "I can guarantee that."

Steve agreed. There was no way someone could've followed them last night without their being aware of it.

"I don't want to be the bad guy here," Derek said. "But, Steve, yesterday you were sure Rosalyn had contacted the Watcher. Are you sure something like that didn't happen again?"

Steve wasn't going back down that road. "Yes, I'm sure. However he's finding her, it's not because she's telling him."

Derek held out his hands in surrender. "All right, don't kill me. All I'm saying is sometimes the simplest answer is the most likely one."

"Well, start looking for complex answers because Rosalyn isn't helping the Watcher." If they had seen her face when she'd found that letter, they wouldn't question it either. Steve would give everything he had to never see that look on Rosalyn's face ever again.

Jon jumped in before things got out of hand. "We need to get Rosalyn back to HQ. You too, Steve. We'll work out the hows and whys from there. And I have some other cases I've found that I think might have an interesting tie to what's happening to Rosalyn."

"Steve, I'm going to open the letter now," Molly called out from the hallway. "I've gotten all the forensic evidence I can from the floor around it and the outside of the envelope."

They all moved into the hallway.

Molly looked up, shaking her head. "I had hoped he had licked the envelope. That would've been our best shot at DNA."

"He never licks the envelope." Rosalyn's voice was tight at the top of the stairs. "Not once. He's too smart for that."

"I was going to read the note." Molly looked up at Rosalyn. "Is that okay?"

Rosalyn nodded.

Molly opened the envelope and her eyes flew to Steve. This had to be bad.

"Go ahead," he murmured.

"'I can't wait to meet your baby. Maybe he'll decide to come live with me. But I'll get rid of Dad first.'"

Rosalyn let out a sob and held on to the banister for support. Steve took the stairs two at a time to get to her, then pulled her hard to his chest. He could feel shudders racking her small frame.

"He'll kill you. He'll take the baby."

"No," he whispered in her ear. "Do you hear me? That maniac will never touch our child. I promise you that. And I can take care of myself."

"Not all the time, you can't. He'll wear you down. That's what he does." Her quiet sobs broke his heart.

He held her close, fury streaming through his blood. He looked down the stairs at Liam and Derek.

"I want to get her back to HQ, now."

Within minutes they were on their way. They left the forensic team and coroner's office representatives, as well as members of the SWAT team. Derek stayed to oversee everything but really to keep an eye on his wife if the Watcher decided to come back for any reason.

Everyone else made a caravan to get Rosalyn back to Omega. Liam was in the car in front of Steve, Jon in the car behind. Weapons hot in case there was any problem. Rosalyn sat in the backseat in Steve's car. Andrea was beside her, arm around her shoulder. Brandon was on the other side.

Every time he caught a glance at Rosalyn's face in the rearview mirror, his heart sank a little more. She was pale to the point of gray, her lips pinched until they were colorless. Her blue eyes, usually so full of life, were dull, lifeless.

Like she had given up.

Steve felt marginally better as they pulled into Omega and he got her into the building. The Watcher's violence seemed to be escalating, and now he was using guns. Rosalyn would be staying inside the Omega compound until they caught the Watcher.

They moved quickly past the security guard, Steve biting his tongue when Rosalyn once again set off the metal detector. The guard ran the wand up the front and back of her body but found nothing.

This was ridiculous. "Get those things looked at," he barked to the guard. The man nodded quickly.

He slipped his arm around Rosalyn, keeping her close to his side as they walked down the hall.

"I need to write this note in my notebook. It's important for me to keep an accurate record. Detective Johnson said so."

Rosalyn's voice sounded unnatural. Distant. Steve shot a concerned look over at Andrea.

"Sure, honey." Andrea rubbed Rosalyn's arm. "Your notebook is in the conference room. I'll help you write it down."

When they got to the room, Jon grabbed Steve's arm. "Brandon and I found something interesting last night after you left."

"Okay."

Brandon and Jon both turned to look at the two women, who were settling in at the conference room table. Jon shook his head. "I'm not sure if it's something we should say in front of Rosalyn. Especially given her fragile state right now."

"Okay, let's go into my office. You can run it by me and then we can decide whether to tell Rosalyn. Although I don't want to keep secrets from her if it's going to affect her safety. More information is better in this case."

Brandon nodded. "I think we both agree. It's some other cases we found that are interesting."

As soon as they were in Steve's office, Brandon pulled out four files. He opened one and laid down a picture of a young woman.

"This is the one I remembered. It's from two years

ago." Brandon's genius mind didn't forget much of anything. It had helped them on cases more than once. "Her
name was Tracy Solheim. From Jackson, Mississippi."

Steve picked up the file and looked over it. "Says
she committed suicide."

Brandon nodded. "She did. She was twenty-one.
But for six months before she killed herself she told
multiple people, her family, friends, even the police,
that she had a stalker. Said she was receiving notes."

"Nobody believed her," Jon continued. "Tracy had
a history of emotional trauma. Did a lot of weird stuff
to get attention over the years. Police reports did say
she had notes but that none of them were threatening
in any way."

Steve shrugged. "Okay, there are some similarities
there. But not enough to convince me it's the same
guy."

Brandon nodded. "I agree. But look at these three
others. One's from Tampa, one's from Birmingham,
Alabama, and one's from New Orleans."

"I'm assuming the point is the radius to Mobile,
Alabama, Rosalyn's hometown."

"It's almost a semicircle," Jon said. "And within
the last six years there's been a woman who has committed suicide in all those cities. All white females
within twenty to twenty-five years of age. All who
complained to family and at least once to the police
about receiving 'strange' notes. In all the cases nothing was done to help them, because they were deemed
nonthreatening."

Brandon pulled out a piece of paper. "This is what
clinched it for me. One of the officers from the New

Orleans case at least wrote down in his official report what some of the notes said."

Brandon had blown them up so they were each on a separate sheet of paper.

The park was nice today, wasn't it?

I would've chosen the red sweater, but the blue one looks nice too.

Did you enjoy dinner with your friends? I was hoping you'd get the shrimp rather than the chicken.

"Those are all similar in tone to some of the notes Rosalyn has quoted in her notebook."

Brandon nodded. "Exactly. And also, innocent enough to not be taken seriously by the police."

Steve sat down in the seat next to the table and leaned back. "Okay, let's assume this is the same guy. So what happened? The Watcher killed them? I thought you said they were suicide."

"Yes, all confirmed suicide." Brandon sat in the other chair. "We think that's his MO, Steve. He drives these women away from their families, away from their loved ones. He isolates them. He's smart enough not to threaten them in the notes, so nothing can be done with the police."

"To what end? He's obviously not living out any fantasies with these women." That was almost always part of a violent stalker's MO—having the women with him. "He's not killing them, right?"

"He's a serial killer, Steve." Jon braced himself on the table with both arms. "Every bit as much as ones that we profile. But instead of using a certain weapon or certain ritual, he pushes and pushes until they do it themselves. That *is* his ritual."

It was so sick and yet made so much sense at the same time.

A serial killer who didn't actually kill his victims. Drove them to killing themselves by isolating them from everyone they loved, by terrorizing them until they felt they had no other choice.

It took a special sort of evil to inflict emotional trauma of that magnitude.

Steve realized the Watcher could've killed Rosalyn at any time. She'd been alone, undefended, for months before she met him and months afterward. The Watcher hadn't tried to harm her. It was only within the last few days that he'd turned violent toward her.

And actually, he really hadn't turned violent toward *her*. True, he'd killed Rosalyn's sister, but probably because he found out it was Lindsey and not Rosalyn. He'd also been trying to kill Steve, not Rosalyn; she'd just been near collateral damage.

Brandon cleared his throat, dragging Steve's attention back into the room. "If you think about it, the fact that Rosalyn is still alive is a testament to her strength. We're still gathering information about these other women, but so far it seems that none of them lasted as long as Rosalyn has."

Steve stood. "Because she was alone a long time before the Watcher found her."

"She doesn't have family?" Brandon's brow wrinkled. "That would go against our profile."

"No, she has family. Just none of them have ever been there for her. She has, in essence, been alone her whole life." Steve began restacking the files. "Let's go tell Rosalyn what we've found. I think it will definitely help, not hurt. At least give her an understanding of what's going on."

Yeah, she'd been alone. But she damn sure wasn't anymore.

Chapter Nineteen

Steve had been correct—telling Rosalyn about Jon and Brandon's theory had been the right thing to do. She felt sad for the other women and angry that the Watcher seemed to be getting away with a horrible crime without anyone even knowing. But mostly she was relieved to finally understand what was happening.

"So he was trying to get me to kill myself." She was sitting across the table from him, next to Andrea. Her voice was still soft but at least she didn't look as fragile as she had before. "I almost did, you know. That night I met you."

"He wanted you to feel that way," Steve said.

"Yes," Brandon agreed. "That's his pattern. From what we can tell, he's very methodical about what he does. Almost like this is some sort of experiment to him. He wants to see how far he can push each woman before she breaks."

Jon nodded. "He's smart. Knows about law enforcement. His notes are never threatening and don't mention anything that would raise a red flag with police."

"Like what?" Rosalyn asked.

"Anything that would show obsession. 'We'll be together forever' sort of stuff. Instead the Watcher mentions normal everyday occurrences. Meals. Activities. Something a friend would mention casually, not someone obsessed."

Steve sat down in a chair across from Rosalyn. "Because he's not obsessed."

Brandon nodded. "Exactly. He's scientific. Experimental. He's not obsessed with the women themselves, just what sort of reactions he can get from them."

"And he doesn't actually harm them himself," Brandon continued. "But he uses tools of psychological terror instead—isolation, fear, imbalance. Then it's just a matter of time before they crack."

"You didn't," Steve told her.

A single tear escaped and rolled slowly down the side of her cheek. "I almost did. If I hadn't met you that night…"

He leaned forward, closer to her. "But you did meet me, not that I was of much help at the time. And if you hadn't, you still would've made it through. You're one of the strongest people I've ever met."

Her smile was breathtaking.

She now knew the Watcher's endgame—her taking her own life—and she was bound and determined not to give it to him. It was all Steve could do not to pull her up into his arms right there in the conference room in front of everyone. She was amazing.

And she was his. She might not realize it, but he had no intention of letting her out of his sight even after this was over. The baby was part of that, true, but he wasn't the only part. Steve wanted Rosalyn—

with all her strength, beauty, radiance—in his life. If she would have him.

"The Watcher doesn't hurt the women," Steve finally said, "but he's obviously not above violence. We've got a dead agent and Rosalyn has a dead sister that proves that. He's a killer."

"Yes, absolutely." Brandon nodded. "But killing the others are him manipulating variables in his equation. A means to an end. I don't think he's killing because he likes it. He's killing to further the reaction in his victims. To isolate them further."

"Everything's different now," Rosalyn looked around the room. "He hasn't got me isolated anymore. But he threatened the baby, Steve."

"That's his way of trying to continue his manipulation of you." Steve squeezed her hand. "There's no way he can get to you here. We'll put protective custody around your mom."

"The Ammonses too. In Georgia," Rosalyn whispered.

Steve nodded. "Roman should be checking in soon. He was meeting with them this morning."

"We've still got a lot of holes," Jon said. "The same ones Brandon was mentioning last night. Mainly, why didn't you hear from the Watcher for the six months you were in Georgia, and how he keeps knowing where you are, even though there aren't any more tracking devices on your clothing. There's no way he should've been able to find you at Steve's house last night."

"I swear I didn't tell him where I was," Rosalyn was quick to interject.

"No one thinks you did," Andrea murmured, leaning closer to Rosalyn.

Steve nodded quickly. "No one is idiot enough to think you're involved."

She raised an eyebrow at him.

He shrugged, grinning sheepishly. "At least not today."

She rolled her eyes. Steve was so happy to see her more lively that he couldn't be the least bit irritated.

When he'd seen the note that threatened their baby... Renewed rage caused Steve's fists to clench. He would make this right no matter what it took.

"We're still looking for other cases," Jon said. "Because of the intensity of his crimes, we're pretty sure he can only stalk one woman at a time, maybe two at the most. None of the cases overlap. There are probably others but we haven't found them yet. And we're still gathering info on the cases we have found."

A call beeped through to the conference room's phone. Steve pressed the speaker button.

"Roman Weber is holding for you, Steve," Cynthia told him. "He's in Ellijay, Georgia."

"Good. Maybe he can provide some answers. Put him through."

"Hey." Roman's voice came through clearly. "Remind me next time you want me to go to some tiny town in Georgia to make you send someone else."

Steve caught the slightest hint of a smile on Rosalyn's face.

"Roman, I have you on speaker in the conference room. Everyone's here."

"I talked to the Ammonses this morning. Like Rosalyn said, they're good people. Just don't trust the government much. Their son died in the military, years ago, but I think they were probably pretty skeptical before that."

"Okay. Did you find anything of interest?"

"I tell you what, these people are more than ready for a TEOTWAWKI event. They've got a cellar full of food, water purifiers, ammunition. You name it."

Rosalyn looked confused. "What does *TEOTWAWKI* mean?"

"The end of the world as we know it," Jon explained. "A lot of survivalists use the term."

"They're definitely off the grid. No computers, only one phone. The whole town is prepared for a zombie apocalypse or whatever, but the Ammonses are definitely the most paranoid."

"Did you talk to them yourself?" Steve asked.

"Yes, they said to give you their best, Rosalyn. And to let you know you are welcome back at any time."

Rosalyn smiled. "If you see them again, send my best too. I know they're not very talkative."

"That's for sure. Steve, in all their survivor gear—and believe me, it's extensive—they have some jamming devices. They didn't want the government listening in on them in any way. This wouldn't stop a lot of the higher-end devices we have now, but it would've protected them from the basics."

And there they had it. One mystery solved. Steve looked at Rosalyn across the table. "And their equipment would have interfered with transmissions of all kinds."

"No doubt. I thought you would find that interesting,

given the transmission devices you found on Rosalyn's clothes."

"Great, Roman," Steve said. "I need you to stay there and keep an eye on the Ammonses. If you're right about everything, there shouldn't be a problem. We think we have a profile on the killer. Doesn't look like he'll be coming your way, but just in case."

"Got it, boss."

Roman gave a little more information before hanging up, promising to keep a watchful eye for anything unusual.

"Well, that solves question one of the two. The Watcher couldn't find you while you were at the Ammonses' because the equipment they were using to block the government from hearing them—not that the government is listening to a couple in their seventies who have never broken the law—also kept the Watcher from being able to hear or find you."

He could see Rosalyn's relief at one more piece of the puzzle falling into place.

"Thank God." She leaned back in her chair. "I was afraid he'd just been toying with me. That he was going to hurt the Ammonses in some way, even though I never mentioned him to them."

"Looks like the Watcher may not know about them at all. Their government paranoia saved them from a serial killer." Steve reached over and grabbed her hand again. He didn't care if anyone else knew about his feelings for Rosalyn. It's not like he'd done such a good job hiding them up to now.

They all took a break to eat lunch. Steve walked with Rosalyn to the small cafeteria in the building. He wanted to make sure she wasn't missing any meals she couldn't afford to miss. He saw her hands suddenly fly to her belly and a little smile cross her face. He knew the baby had kicked again.

It just made him all the more determined to keep them safe.

But to do that they had to figure out how the Watcher was finding them now.

Back in the conference after lunch, they pored over the case files, comparing what little dates and specific information they had to Rosalyn's much more in-depth notebook. Jon and Brandon had already left, Jon to Tampa, Brandon to New Orleans, to see if they could gather more intel from talking to the victims' families and the local police.

They wouldn't give the families all the details in the cases, especially since right now it was only a theory, but they would let them know that there had been others who had suffered similar fates. Maybe there would be something—or someone—else the family members could remember.

Andrea worked with Joe Matarazzo to see if they could find any ties between the other four victims and Rosalyn. They'd shown Rosalyn all the women's pictures, but she hadn't recognized any of them.

Steve couldn't stay with Rosalyn the entire day like he wanted to. He had to deal with Doug Wilson's death; the tragic job of notifying the family belonged to him. He also had to catch up the local PD with what had happened at his house this morning.

He wanted Rosalyn's case to be the only thing he had to work on, but it couldn't be.

When he got back to the conference room at nearly nine o'clock that evening, she was still poring over her notes with Andrea and Joe.

"Time for everyone to go home," he announced. "We'll pick up fresh tomorrow."

Joe nodded before hugging both women. Steve wasn't offended or threatened. Joe was a people person to his very core.

"Tomorrow, boss," he said on his way out.

"Tell Laura I said hello." Steve and Laura, Joe's bride, had become close since they both were almost burned alive by a psychopath a few months ago.

"I'm sure she's going to want you to come to dinner with your new girlfriend." Joe said it in an exaggerated stage whisper, winking at Steve.

Steve's eyes met Rosalyn's. She was shaking her head at Joe's antics, as they all tended to do.

"I'll see you guys tomorrow too," Andrea said as she put her blazer back on. She hugged Rosalyn. "We'll start again first thing. Welcome to real-life police work. It takes time."

Rosalyn's frustration colored all her features as she looked down at the case files and papers spread out all over the table. It wasn't messy but it was chaotic.

He slipped an arm around her shoulders and pulled her to his side. "Andrea's right, you know. It takes time."

She eased against him but rubbed her face with her hands. "We've gone over so much my brain hurts. And I don't know that we're any closer to catching the Watcher."

"We are. Every day we put together more of the puzzle pieces. Soon we'll have a good view overall."

"I can't stay here forever. He has me just as much trapped here as he did when he had me on the run before."

He grabbed her by both shoulders so they could look eye to eye.

"No. You're not alone here. You have people who will do whatever it takes to keep you safe. We will catch him, Rosalyn."

She shrugged. "I hope so. Everyone has lives they need to get on with. They can't spend all their time just on this one case."

He pulled her to his chest and felt her arms wrap around his waist.

"You let me worry about that. Working cases, hunting down people who hurt others? That's what we do here. We find the patterns nobody else sees. And we're damn good at our job."

"Okay." She nodded her head against his chest.

"We'll catch him." He brought his lips down to her forehead. "I will do whatever it takes to make sure you and our baby are safe. I promise you that."

It was a promise he had every intention of keeping.

Chapter Twenty

Rosalyn awoke to sounds of voices in the small living room area of the Omega Sector apartment. Evidently the apartment was used by experts who came to help with cases or by agents who needed a night's rest and didn't want to go to their homes.

Or for people who were being hunted by psychopaths.

The apartment was within the compound but outside the main section of offices. Members of the SWAT team, angry over the death of an Omega agent, were taking turns guarding the door. Ashton Fitzgerald had been there when she and Steve had arrived.

Rosalyn had fallen to sleep knowing the Watcher couldn't find her here. Or at least couldn't get to her.

But she had dreamed that he sat right outside the gate. In a lawn chair. Drinking coffee and reading a newspaper. His face was hidden from her in some sort of unnatural darkness, but she could clearly see a giant knife sitting on a small table by his side.

Just waiting for her to exit Omega so he could kill her.

Worse than that, the bodies of everyone she'd come

to know and care about at Omega Sector—Jon, Brandon, Andrea, Derek, Joe—lay around him. Murdered.

Steve's body sat propped up closer to the Watcher, blood staining his T-shirt. Steve's green eyes were open, lifeless, staring out blankly.

Rosalyn took a step outside the gate. The Watcher folded his paper and stood.

"I was beginning to think you'd never come out of there," he said, his voice sounding like it was coming through one of those modulator things. "But I had fun with your friends since you were so busy protecting yourself."

She watched in horror as he kicked Steve's body over and rushed toward her.

"I'm so excited to meet the baby!"

She'd awakened sobbing right before he reached her.

Steve had held her in the bed as she fought him at first—caught in the terror of her dream—then as she sobbed.

"You're all going to die because of me. Because I'm hiding and the Watcher wants to keep his sick game moving forward."

"Nobody else is going to die. We are all on high alert and everyone can handle themselves."

He'd stroked her hair and held her close to his chest, murmuring soft words of comfort and encouragement. But she still couldn't fall back asleep until the light of dawn crept up through the small window.

She heard the deep timbre of Steve's voice right away and soon recognized the other voices to be Derek and Molly Waterman. Maybe Molly had found something when analyzing the crime scene at Steve's house yesterday. Rosalyn got dressed and went out into the small living room. She didn't have any makeup to put on even if she could have been bothered to do so.

Steve immediately crossed to her and kissed her on her forehead.

"You okay?" He led her over to the small kitchen island so she could have something to eat and some coffee. "I'll make you eggs and toast."

"Thank you. Rough dreams, but yeah, I'm okay now." She turned to Molly and Derek. "Good morning. Anything new?"

Molly surprised her by coming over to give her a hug. It had been a long time since she'd had friends, really anyone besides Steve, who cared about her. She returned Molly's hug, trying not to be as awkward as she felt.

"We didn't find anything useful at Steve's house. Like you said about the other notes, there was no usable DNA available."

Rosalyn swallowed and nodded. She hadn't really expected them to find anything. "I'm not surprised. I had hoped maybe a professional would find something I had overlooked all these times."

Molly shook her head. "There was nothing to be found, not by you, not by anyone. I'm sure that was true for the other notes, as well."

Rosalyn felt a little bit better.

"But Jon found a transmitter on an article of clothing of one of the other deceased victims. He's bringing it back here so I can analyze it."

Steve looked over from where he was cooking at the stove. "Our primary focus with your case as of now is figuring out how the Watcher has found you after we removed the trackers in Pensacola."

"Being able to look at a functional transmitter will help me," Molly said. "I might be able to pinpoint where it was made."

Steve fed not only Rosalyn but Derek and Molly breakfast. Molly and Derek told humorous stories of Molly's own pregnancy—their daughter had been born five months ago—and some of Derek's outrageous behavior in the delivery room.

Evidently the big, bad SWAT agent who towered over his petite wife had been reduced to "less than useless"—Molly's words—while their child made her entry into the world.

"It was time to go to the hospital, and he got lost." Molly rolled her eyes. "The man navigated his way through a Colombian jungle once to rescue me and he couldn't figure out how to get to a hospital eight miles away."

Derek nearly choked on his piece of toast. "I made one wrong turn. That is not the same as getting lost."

She slapped him on the back to help with his coughing. "Of course, honey." She turned to Rosalyn. "He was lost," Molly said in an exaggerated sigh.

Steve laughed.

"Just you wait." Derek stabbed some of his eggs, glaring at Steve. "Your time is coming. I'm going to follow you around with a camera."

The normal conversation, the joking, even the glares,

made Rosalyn feel better. Made life seem a little more normal.

But then the vision of the Watcher in her dream came back.

If the Watcher killed Molly and Derek, their daughter would be an orphan. Rosalyn fought to keep down the food she'd just eaten.

Steve moved closer to her. "Whatever you're thinking right now, stop," he whispered in her ear as Derek and Molly gathered her papers so they could all leave.

"But…"

Steve tilted her chin up. "I know it feels this way to you, but the Watcher is not the baddest bad guy we've ever faced. Isn't that right, Derek?"

"Not even in the top ten," Derek confirmed.

"That man is not going to let anything happen to Molly, so don't even let that enter your mind."

"Nope." Derek confirmed again, reaching down to wrap both arms around his wife's hips and lift her so he could kiss her. "Never again."

"And I'm not going to let anything happen to you."

They got the rest of what they would need for the day and the four of them walked out the door and down the hall. Rosalyn tried to hold on to the good feeling she'd had for a few minutes, but it was lost in the weight of what was happening.

They had to go through the security section again as they entered the main offices. Everyone made it through the metal detector without it going off but Rosalyn. Again. Always her luck.

The poor guy looked as though he feared for his

job when he used the wand on Rosalyn and she set it off once more.

"Eastburn, I thought I told you to get that wand checked." Steve spoke through his teeth with forced restraint.

"Yes, sir, this is a new wand. There shouldn't be any problem with it."

"So, you're suggesting that Ms. Mellinger has a weapon in her mouth?" That was where the wand kept beeping.

"No, sir. I'm not sure what is wrong."

"You ever have problems in airports or anything?" Steve asked her.

Rosalyn shook her head. "I haven't been in one for a few years, but no, not that I recall."

Molly put the files she'd been carrying down and walked over to Steve and Rosalyn. "You've set off the metal detector every time you've come through?"

"Yes." Rosalyn shrugged. "Well, the first time I was in handcuffs, so I'm pretty sure that did it. Yesterday we were assuming it was just a defective wand."

Molly, Derek and Steve were all giving each other looks.

"What?" Rosalyn asked.

Steve tossed some keys to Derek, who put them in his pocket. Steve took the wand from the guard and scanned Derek. It beeped when it got to his pocket, signifying the presence of the keys.

Without Steve asking, Derek took the keys out of his pocket and handed them to Molly. Steve scanned Derek again, with no beeps this time.

"Scanner seems to work correctly," Derek said. They all turned and looked at Rosalyn.

"What?" she asked again.

"I need you to come with me over to the lab," Molly said.

"Why?" Rosalyn had no idea what was going on.

"We need to take an X-ray of your mouth. Your teeth in particular. I think we've just discovered how the Watcher keeps finding you."

ONCE MOLLY MADE her announcement, everyone flurried into action. Rosalyn wasn't quite sure what to do except go along with it.

"The X-ray equipment in the lab is not really for use on a human," Molly stated as she walked with Steve and Rosalyn toward the lab. Derek had gone to research transmitters.

"Is it safe for the baby?" Steve asked. "I won't risk any harm to Rosalyn or the baby just for quicker results. If we need to get her to a hospital, we can make that work safely."

"No X-ray machine is great for any human. It's radiation. But it's a small amount for a very short time. And we'll use a lead covering." Molly turned to Rosalyn and took her hand. "Under the same circumstances, I would've allowed the X-ray when I was pregnant. That's the best assurance I can give you."

Rosalyn nodded. It was enough.

Molly's comfort inside her lab was evident. She slipped on a white coat and began giving orders and answering questions the moment she arrived. Obviously how things occurred here every day.

Molly led them into a smaller room with an X-ray machine. "We're fortunate. We got the X-ray as part of the new lab."

Rosalyn looked over at Steve as Molly set up the machine so it could be used on her rather than objects.

"New lab?"

Steve nodded. "About eighteen months ago a terrorist group bombed the lab to try to hide some evidence concerning a bigger crime. We rebuilt a newer, better one."

"I'm glad you weren't in here when it blew, Molly."

"Me too. We did lose one tech, though." Rosalyn saw the glance between Molly and Steve. There was more to this story than they were saying. She was about to ask when Molly brought her over to sit on a step stool.

She arranged the X-ray machine while Rosalyn held her head in an awkward position. Like Molly had said, the machine wasn't meant for humans. But in the end, they got what they wanted. Ten minutes later they were sitting around Molly's computer as the X-ray image came up.

"There." Molly pointed to one of Rosalyn's teeth from the X-ray.

"My tooth?"

"No. It's a crown. And beyond that, it's a transmitting and locating device. It's how the Watcher has been finding you."

Chapter Twenty-One

They were out in the hall talking about her. As soon as Molly announced about the transmitter, Steve and Molly had immediately stopped talking. It took Rosalyn a minute to understand why.

They were afraid the Watcher could hear everything they were saying.

Steve wrote her a note explaining that, but Rosalyn had already figured out that he and Molly weren't just being rude.

Meanwhile, Rosalyn was fighting the urge to find some sort of pliers and yank the crown out of her jaw.

The Watcher had a transmitter *inside* her body. Rosalyn laughed out loud, although she could recognize the hysteria that tinged it.

All these weeks when she thought the Watcher was inside her head she'd been literally right.

She glanced around for pliers again. Yeah, it would hurt, but the pain might be worth knowing he was out of her thoughts once and for all. But she couldn't find anything in the lab.

Steve and Molly came back in about ten minutes later.

"It's okay—we can talk." Steve came to stand in front of her, putting his hands on her shoulders and rubbing them gently.

"But can't he hear us? The transmitter?" Rosalyn fought to keep her voice even.

"No. Not here at Omega. We use a similar jamming device as the Ammonses use in Georgia. We want to make sure criminals are not privy to our private conversations."

Molly looked up from where she had sat down at her computer. "And ours are on a much greater scale and more sophisticated than the jammers in Georgia. Anything you say here is safe."

Steve wrapped an arm around her shoulder. "Let's go up to the conference room. We need to get Jon and Brandon on a conference call and figure out our next step."

"I want to get it out as soon as possible," she told both of them. "Fortunately, I couldn't find a pair of pliers while you were in the hallway talking or I might have already taken care of it myself."

"Absolutely," Steve agreed. "I want that thing out of you just as much, believe me."

"It's still a crown. It's cemented in," Molly reminded them. "A dentist will be much less painful and ready for any emergency."

She and Steve were both deep in their own thoughts as they made it back to the conference room. He had Brandon and Jon on the line within minutes, explaining what they'd found.

"That makes so much sense," Brandon said. "The

reason why he could find Rosalyn at Steve's house but can't find her at Omega."

"Yes," Steve agreed. "Molly and I already double-checked. Omega's frequency jammer is keeping the signal from being broadcast any farther than the building."

"So he probably has no idea where you are, Rosalyn," Jon said.

"That's right," Steve agreed. "And even if he somehow followed her, there's no way he can get in."

She felt safe, but she still wanted the thing out of her mouth.

"More important," Brandon said, "this gives us a big clue as to who the Watcher is."

Steve turned to her. "Your dentist, Rosalyn. There's no way that transmitter could've been put in the crown by accident. Whoever did your dental work is most likely the Watcher."

"Fits the profile," Jon agreed. "Intelligent. Professional. My personal bet had been on some sort of doctor, but I guess a dentist is close enough. Plus, he would've had days he could devote to following you and days he couldn't, thus the gap in notes sometimes."

Of course. Rosalyn felt a little stupid that she hadn't thought of that immediately.

"I'm going to bet you had that done about a year ago?" Brandon asked.

"Yes." Rosalyn sat down in one of the conference room chairs. "I don't like going to the dentist. So I found one who would put me under general anesthesia to do the root canal."

She looked at Steve. "Actually, my sister was the

one who told me about him. I think he practices all over the Southeast. Gunson was his last name. I don't remember his first."

Steve reached down and kissed her on the forehead. "That's enough. We'll get him now."

CHRISTOPHER GUNSON DIDN'T know it, but his days as a free man were numbered.

Even without the first name it hadn't taken long for them to find him. His primary practice was based out of Mobile, but he also did work in New Orleans.

It said so right there on his website. The website also explained that he understood the fear people had of dentists, that the fear wasn't unreasonable. That he would rather work with patients by whatever means necessary—including general anesthesia for procedures—than for them not to have dental care at all.

It was easy to see how he drew patients in. And then, when they were out cold for their procedures, he could easily place a transmitter and tracking device like he had in Rosalyn's mouth.

Brandon was on his way to Gunson's New Orleans office right now. Jon was flying from Tampa to Mobile to investigate the practice there.

Steve didn't expect them to find the man at either site, because he was sure Gunson was still here in Colorado. He might not know where Rosalyn was exactly, since he couldn't track her or listen to her while she was in the Omega building, but Steve had no doubt he would be waiting to make a move as soon as she wasn't in their protection.

They hadn't found a good picture of Gunson on his

website. The most recent picture they had was taken of him ten years ago at a dental convention in Las Vegas.

In the picture he was in his late thirties, already balding and pretty thick around the middle. Steve imagined the ten years since hadn't been kind. He wondered if that was the reason Gunson stalked women. If it gave him a sense of power he didn't otherwise have in real life.

Maybe he wasn't so different from the average stalker, after all.

Rosalyn was holding it together, but barely. Every time he looked over at her, she was rubbing her jaw where the transmitter was. She wanted it out and he didn't blame her. But they couldn't do it here. And right now it was more important that they make their move on Gunson, before he realized they were onto him.

Once the transmitter was gone from her mouth, Gunson would know his identity was blown.

So as long as Rosalyn wasn't in a panic, they needed to leave it in. At least for a few more hours.

Steve wished he could distract her. Take her back upstairs to the apartment and let her rest. He knew she hadn't slept very well last night.

But he couldn't. He was coordinating with both the New Orleans and Mobile Police Departments to provide back up when Brandon and Jon arrived. They needed to make sure nobody got a call in to Gunson once they raided the offices. They had to collect as much information as they could without clueing in Gunson.

A few hours later Steve received the call. Brandon and the New Orleans police had moved in on Gunson's office. Gunson had surprised everyone by actually being there, in his office, with patients. Definitely not in Colorado. The locals took him into custody and allowed Brandon to use their facilities to interrogate him and were providing Omega with the live feed of the questioning.

As soon as Steve saw the man through the monitor—and Steve had been right; the ten years hadn't been kind to him—crying, before Brandon even asked a question, Steve knew this wasn't the Watcher.

But still he hoped.

Rosalyn sat next to him watching the screen too.

"Yes," she whispered. "That's Dr. Gunson. He's really the Watcher?"

"Let's see what Brandon can find out."

Gunson had already been read his rights but hadn't insisted on an attorney. Probably not a smart move on his part.

Also another clue that he probably wasn't the killer. Steve grimaced.

But if anybody had to be in there questioning him, Brandon Han was the perfect person. His ability to get inside the minds of criminals was unparalleled. Brandon might not be able to get a confession, but he would definitely walk out of there with a pretty damn educated guess about Gunson's involvement.

Andrea came running into the room. "Brandon's about to interview Gunson?"

"Yeah." Steve gestured to the seat beside Rosalyn. "Join us, please. Give us your opinion."

They all tuned in to the screen.

"Can you tell me why you're crying, Dr. Gunson?" Brandon's voice was even, nonthreatening.

"I didn't want to do it."

Rosalyn strained closer to the screen.

"Didn't want to do what, Christopher? Is it okay if I call you that? But I don't mind calling you Dr. Gunson, if that's what you prefer. A title of respect."

"That's my man," Andrea murmured. "He always knows the best route to take."

And in this case showing regard to a person feeling dejected was that route.

"Christopher is fine. Or Chris."

"Okay, Chris. Tell me what you didn't want to do."

"I had gotten into financial trouble. Done too much online betting. Lost too much. I was about to lose my house. My practice. Everything."

The crimes against Rosalyn hadn't been of any financial gain, the opposite, in fact. He would probably lose money being away from his practice to follow the women.

Brandon had to know that, but he didn't let it show. Instead he nodded. "So you did something you shouldn't."

"The transmitters. I knew they were wrong."

Steve heard Rosalyn's soft gasp at Gunson's admission.

Gunson sat back in his seat, defeated. At least he wasn't crying anymore. "I really don't know much. I didn't want to know what he was studying. I didn't want to know how it worked or anything about the transmitters themselves."

"Someone paid you to put transmitters in dental work."

"He's not the Watcher," Rosalyn murmured.

Steve squeezed her shoulder, keeping his frustration at bay. He'd wanted this to be over. Wanted Rosalyn to be able to walk out of here completely free of the Watcher.

That wasn't going to happen today unless Gunson had a lot more info than he was letting on.

"Who paid you, Chris?" Brandon leaned in toward the other man.

"I don't know. I never met him face-to-face. About six years ago I was really in deep with some loan sharks. They were going to break my fingers."

Gunson looked at Brandon as if that explained everything. Brandon gestured for him to continue.

"So when a man approached me and said he was doing some unorthodox experimentation and needed me to put some transmitters into crowns, I finally broke down and did it."

"How many transmitters have you put in in those six years, Chris?"

"I don't know."

"He's lying about that," Andrea said. "Everything else he's been telling the truth about. But about this he's lying."

"How do you know he's lying?" Rosalyn asked.

"The way he looked down and to the left."

"I didn't even see him look anywhere." Rosalyn leaned closer to the screen.

"Andrea is very good at what she does, sweetheart. Don't feel bad—I didn't see it either."

"Brandon did," Andrea murmured. "I can tell."

Brandon leaned in toward Gunson. "Chris, this is only going to work if we're honest with each other. I think you know how many transmitters you put in patients' mouths. That's not something you would forget."

"Twenty-nine," Gunson finally responded. "All women. Over six years. He paid me $10,000 for each one."

Rosalyn sat ramrod straight and Steve sucked a breath through his teeth. Twenty-nine women had transmitters in their teeth. So far, including Rosalyn, they knew of five. And four of them were dead.

They watched as Brandon showed the pictures of the dead women. Gunson remembered each. Brandon didn't tell him the women were dead, a good call since the dentist seemed to be holding on by a thin thread anyway.

Brandon confirmed that Gunson had been in town the last forty-eight hours. The man gave a detailed report of what he'd done and with whom. Brandon would follow up, of course, but there was no doubt in Steve's mind.

Christopher Gunson wasn't the Watcher. He was pathetic and would be going to jail, but he wasn't the Watcher.

He could tell Rosalyn knew it too. When she looked back at him, devastation was clearly written across her face.

The worst news hit them at the very end. Brandon asked for information about the other patients. These women, even if they had never been contacted by the

Watcher, even if their transmitters weren't live, needed to know what had happened to them.

Gunson looked ashamed as he explained that once the procedure had been done, he had given the patient records over to the man in order to receive payments. Although Gunson recognized the pictures of the women Brandon had shown him, he could not provide the names or any information about the other women he'd performed the procedure on.

They still had no idea who the Watcher was. All they knew was that he had two dozen other victims to whom he could turn his attention at any time.

If he hadn't already.

Chapter Twenty-Two

Rosalyn dreamed of the Watcher again that night.

He was still waiting outside the fence of Omega, tossing something small up in the air and then catching it as it came back down. Rosalyn didn't have to be able to see it to know it was a transmitter.

All the Omega agents lay dead around him again. Rosalyn tried not to look at them, knowing she'd never make it if she did.

Make it where? Away from the Watcher? She could go now. He wouldn't be able to follow her.

But now not only did the Watcher have all the Omega agents, he had twenty-eight women tied up in chairs. Blindfolded. Helpless.

Four were obviously dead.

He walked up and down the line of the other women as if he was trying to decide who to choose next.

Rosalyn woke up sobbing again.

"Hey, it's okay."

Steve. He was here, holding her again like he had last night.

"He's going to kill those women. There are twenty-four other women and he's going to kill them. Or get them to kill themselves."

Steve pulled her closer. "We'll stop him."

"How? Dr. Gunson doesn't have any idea who he is."

"We know his pattern now. His MO. We'll catch him, Rosalyn. This is what we do."

"But more women will die first."

Steve was silent for a moment. "Not necessarily. We'll do whatever it takes to keep that from happening."

Rosalyn twisted around, forcing Steve onto his back so she could see his face in the dim light of the moon through the small window. "I'm your best shot at keeping that from happening."

"Why do you say that?"

"If we leave the transmitter in my mouth, we can use it to catch him."

"No. I know how much that thing bothers you. It bothers me too. I don't want him having the means of finding you." He pulled her closer to his side and put his lips against her forehead. "The dentist is coming in the morning. The transmitter comes out. We'll see if it can be salvaged and still used, but your part ends there."

She snuggled into his side. It felt good to have someone care about her. To have someone she could lean on literally and figuratively.

"Go back to sleep," he whispered.

Rosalyn's eyes drifted closed but she knew she would still see the Watcher's other victims when sleep claimed her.

THEY HAD DEEMED it safer to bring a dentist in rather than have Rosalyn go out where she could be tracked.

Once they had the transmitter out of her mouth, Steve hoped to be able to use it to trick the Watcher in some way. To trap him.

Molly had offered one of the rooms in her lab for the dentist to do his work. Rosalyn was less than thrilled with dentists in general—thus how she'd gotten into this mess in the first place—and the thought of one working on her while she sat in a reclinable office chair did not reassure her.

But she wanted the transmitter out. Wanted to know for sure her baby was safe.

She took one look in the room where the dentist was setting up and knew she couldn't do it. But not because of her fear of the dentist.

Because she knew if she had this transmitter taken out of her tooth now, she wouldn't be able to help stop the Watcher.

"Everything okay?" Molly stepped up to her as Rosalyn stood paralyzed in the door. "I know this looks a little rough. But you won't be able to feel anything once he gets you numb."

"I can't do it."

She felt Molly's hand rubbing her back. "Dr. Mitchell is an excellent dentist, I promise you. It won't hurt."

"No, it's not because of the dentist. Believe me, I want this thing out of me enough to probably let him go at me with no numbing at all. It's the Watcher. This is our best link to him. To stopping him."

Molly nodded. "That's another reason we chose Dr. Mitchell. He's one of the most likely people to be able to get the transmitter out intact."

"The Watcher listens to me with the transmitter,

right? I mean, it tells him where I am, but he also physically hears my voice."

"Yes, from what I can tell from the X-ray."

"So if we take it out of my mouth, he's going to know something's different, right? He's going to be able to tell."

"Rosalyn..."

"If I get this removed, I'm making myself safe, but we'll lose our best chance of catching him."

Molly shook her head. "We'll find another way of catching him. You don't need to risk your life. Risk your mental health."

But Rosalyn had already made up her mind. "I'm not going to let another woman go through what I've gone through. Not if it's in my power to stop him."

Molly spent a few more minutes making sure that was what Rosalyn really wanted, but Rosalyn knew it was. She couldn't live with herself if more women got hurt.

She wanted to take this bastard down.

Molly escorted Rosalyn back to the conference room. Steve was there. Jon and Brandon had made their way back from the interviews in Mobile and New Orleans. Derek and Ashton Fitzgerald from SWAT were there also.

They were coming up with a plan. Everyone stopped talking when she and Molly entered.

Steve rushed to her. "Hey, are you done already? That took a lot less time than I th—"

"I decided not to do it," she told him.

Steve grabbed her arm gently and backed her up so they could have a more private conversation in the hall. "Last night we agreed for you to get the transmitter out."

Rosalyn looked down at his arm where it gripped her shoulder. He'd rolled up his sleeves as he was working and she could see the bruises from when the Watcher had hit him at the gas station.

"I can't let him hurt someone else."

"We will stop him. That's our job, Rosalyn. Not yours."

"No." She gently kissed his wrist, then ducked under his arm and into the conference room.

She crossed to the head of the table. "The best shot we have of catching him is if the transmitter is still in my mouth and we use me to set him up."

Steve wasn't willing to let it go. He came and stood beside her. "We already have a plan. We'll use an agent of your general build and coloring—probably Lillian here—" he pointed to a woman at the table "—to impersonate you. We'll give the transmitter to her and put her somewhere, he'll follow it and we'll catch him."

Derek nodded, supporting Steve. "Using a trained agent rather than you is a better tactical position for us."

Rosalyn shook her head. "That's assuming the dentist can get the transmitter out unharmed, which is no guarantee."

"Dr. Mitchell is one of the best oral surgeons in the state," Steve said.

Rosalyn rolled her eyes. "And I'm sure he's had lots of practice taking transmitters out of crowns, because that happens so often. No matter how good he is at normal dental stuff, he's never done anything like this before. You can't deny it's a huge risk."

Steve crossed his arms over his chest. "It's an acceptable one."

Everyone was looking at her now. "Even if we get the transmitter out safely, the Watcher is still going to know something is different. He can hear my voice. Has months of practice listening. He'll know if my voice is different."

Derek looked at Molly, "Can anything be done after the removal of the transmitter to make it sound like it's still in?"

"I can manipulate it somewhat, but it would just be a guess. I agree with Rosalyn about the sound. After all the time he's spent listening to her, he would notice a difference."

"I agree," Jon said. "Part of the thrill for the Watcher is probably listening in to the women. He wants to think of it all as just a science experiment that he's controlling, but listening probably gives him some measure of sexual thrill."

"And he would definitely be aware of changes," Brandon agreed. "He knows not only the sound of Rosalyn's voice but the pitch and the patterns."

Rosalyn couldn't help the shudder that ran through her.

"It's probably part of how he's known what buttons to press to get the biggest reactions out of his victims," Brandon continued. "He studied their voice patterns to see what caused the stress and then preyed on that."

Rosalyn nodded, trying not to lose her nerve. "So we all agree that taking it out is not the best thing to do."

Everyone around the table began talking at once. There was no clear consensus about the best plan.

Steve held up a hand to quiet everyone. He turned to Derek. "Derek, you and Ashton and the rest of SWAT will be heading up most of the sting. What's your opinion?"

Derek leaned back in his chair. "It's never my first choice to put a civilian in the line of fire. A pregnant one makes the situation even more complicated."

Rosalyn refused to be cast aside because of what *might* happen. "But…"

Derek held up his hand in a gesture that encouraged her to let him finish. "But I agree with what you're saying about the transmitter. The Watcher knows your voice. Changes now might spook him."

"We can use you to give all the verbal cues," Ashton said from his place beside Derek. "Then use a replacement agent in the actual location where we plan to arrest him."

Steve looked over at Derek. "You agree?"

Derek shrugged and nodded. "I understand you wanting to keep Rosalyn completely out of this, boss, truly I do. But she's right. Using her is our best bet at catching this guy before he hurts someone else. And if we use Ashton's plan, the risk to Rosalyn is minimal."

Rosalyn reached over and touched Steve's arm, bringing his attention to her. "I want to do this. I *need* to do this."

"And I need to keep you safe. Keep the baby safe."

"We will be safe. You'll be there to protect us every step of the way."

She knew Steve understood. Knew he knew this was the best plan. But she could also understand his hesitancy.

"Fine." He turned back to everyone. "But we don't leave here until we have a plan with no holes. And time is of the essence. Rosalyn has been out of the Watcher's ear for over two and a half days. If we wait too much longer, we'll lose him for good."

Rosalyn knew if that happened, they might never find him again.

Chapter Twenty-Three

"I'll keep hunting him, Rosalyn. We know he's here in the Colorado Springs area because of the note at my house. But I don't think you should leave."

"I don't want to leave you, Steve. We just found each other again. But I have to. We can't be together."

Even knowing the words were fake—an act of theater put on for the Watcher's benefit—Steve didn't like them.

They were about a mile away from the Omega offices. Nothing blocked the transmitter now. The Watcher should be able to hear everything they were saying.

Rosalyn sat inside a café. In the very back corner in a booth. She was huddled down near the table as if she was cold, but really she'd been told to keep her head down in case the Watcher decided to change his MO and take a shot at her.

There were three exits in this café—a front door, a window in the bathroom and the back delivery door. Every person in the building, from the waitstaff to the cooks to the customers, were Omega Sector employees. Not all were active agents, but all were trusted.

Steve wasn't sure exactly how they'd gotten the café

completely emptied in the three hours since they'd finished their planning in the conference room. Steve had asked Joe for a favor, something he'd never asked Joe in the six years he'd known him. He'd asked Joe to use his money and connections to find them a building to pull this off in a ridiculously short amount of time.

Joe hadn't even blinked an eye. He'd called Deacon Crandall, Joe's sort of jack-of-all-trades, and next thing Steve knew, they had a café that could be used for the next week for anything Omega needed. Maybe Joe had used some of his millions of dollars and bought or rented the place; maybe he had just smiled prettily for the owner; who knew? Joe had a way with people. And Deacon was just a man who got stuff done.

Steve wanted to control as many circumstances as he possibly could. He already had a bad feeling in his gut about this situation. But maybe he would have that in any situation that might jeopardize a pregnant civilian.

The building was surrounded by four snipers. Ashton Fitzgerald, by far the best long-range shooter Steve had ever known, had the restaurant in his sights. He wouldn't let anything happen to Rosalyn there.

Steve couldn't be in the café with her. This had to be a telephone call between them for it to work. They didn't plan on it being long enough for the Watcher to get a bead on her location right now. Just enough to get him here tomorrow, when they'd be ready for him. Steve was watching the entire scene from multiple camera angles at the home base inside Omega. But still he itched to be there with Rosalyn. Didn't like having her so far out of his reach.

But he trusted his team.

"You don't need to leave." Steve continued their scripted conversation. "I'll track him down. Just give me more time."

"I can't risk you, Steve. He almost killed you on the motorcycle. If you hadn't turned in time—"

The emotion in Rosalyn's voice was real. And he could see it on her face in the monitor.

"But I did. And I'm okay."

"But how long before the Watcher tries again? I can't take the chance. I have to go."

"No, Rosalyn, just tell me where you are. Where you've been for the past two days."

This was part of the plan. To assure the Watcher they didn't know about the transmitter in her tooth. To make sure Omega wasn't part of his thought process.

"Just at a hotel."

"You're not safe at a hotel. He might find you."

"I'm not safe at your house either, Steve. He found me there."

Steve pulled from his own frustration at not being there next to Rosalyn and put it in his tone. "I can protect you. The Colorado Springs Police Department can protect you."

Steve and Rosalyn realized that they had never talked about Omega outside the Omega building itself. Therefore, the Watcher would not know Steve worked for the multifaceted law enforcement agency. They would convince him Steve was just a member of Colorado Springs PD.

A lone member with no real backup.

"Did you tell your bosses there about the Watcher?"

Steve waited a beat. "Yes."

He could see Rosalyn stir her coffee on the screen. "They didn't believe you, did they?"

"Look, just tell me where you are."

"I can't right now, Steve."

Jon pointed at his watch. They needed to wrap this up. Not give the Watcher enough time to find her today. It had to be tomorrow, when they were ready.

"When are you leaving?"

"Tomorrow. I'm taking a bus. That worked before and the Watcher didn't find me for a long time. I'm hoping that will work again."

"Okay, well, just meet me for breakfast or coffee or something before you go, okay? I just want to see you. To feel the baby kick one more time. You might have him before I can catch the Watcher."

"Okay, fine. My bus leaves at 9:45 a.m. tomorrow."

"Good. Let's meet at eight."

"Fine. There's a little café I'll meet you at." Rosalyn gave him the name and directions to the place she was at now.

"I'll see you tomorrow, sweetheart."

"Be careful, Steve. I don't want anything to happen to you."

Then she clicked the off button.

Steve tapped his communication button to Derek's earpiece. "Okay, get her out of there."

Derek was wearing an apron, posing as a cook in the back. He could see the entire seating area from where he stood.

"Roger that. Everyone in here is still Omega."

Steve watched on the screen as Derek nodded to Lillian, a SWAT team member no less deadly just because she stood barely over five feet tall. She brought Rosalyn a bill. "Here's your check, ma'am."

"Thank you." Rosalyn made a wincing sound as if she was in pain.

"Are you okay?"

"Just my tooth. Something's wrong. But I hate going to the dentist, you know?"

Hopefully the Watcher would buy that there was something wrong with the transmitter. It would force him to move up any timetable he had. To come after Rosalyn tomorrow even if he wasn't planning to. To make a mistake.

"I hope you feel better." Lillian touched the check. "I can take that whenever you're ready."

"Thank you."

That was the agreed-upon code that it was time for Rosalyn to leave. Steve watched as she got up and went out the front door and around to a car in the side parking lot. The camera lost her then, but he knew from there she would drive, as if she was looking for a tail.

Just like she always had done before she'd known how the Watcher was following her. Four different Omega vehicles would be following her, piggybacking off each other so they wouldn't get made. Once they gave her the signal that she was clear, she would drive immediately to Omega, where the transmitter would once again be jammed.

The Watcher would think he'd lost her again for whatever reason. Maybe it was the mountains, or maybe the transmitter itself was faulty—after all, he hadn't had a signal from her the entire time she'd lived with the Ammonses. But hopefully he wouldn't decide to dig too far into it tonight.

But Steve didn't feel like he could draw a complete breath until Rosalyn made it safely back through the gates of Omega. As soon as a member of SWAT brought her up to the offices, Steve pulled her to him, breathing in the scent of her hair.

"How do you think it went? Do you think he bought it?" she asked.

"I hope so."

Jon walked out of the control room. "You did great, Rosalyn. If he doesn't buy it, it's definitely not because of anything you did or didn't do."

She looked up at Steve. "I just want this to be over with."

He kissed her forehead. "Tomorrow it will be."

But Steve knew that even the most well-thought-out plans, the no-holes plans, could sometimes fail.

THE NEXT MORNING all the Omega Sector employees were back at the café. They opened the restaurant at 7:00 a.m. as if they had been doing it for years.

Derek was in the back again as a cook. Jon was in the command room, but it was a van parked around the corner rather than at Omega. He would be calling the shots today, having the bird's-eye view of everything.

Steve had a different role to play: concerned lover.

It didn't require much acting on his part.

Steve would arrive at 7:45 a.m. Rosalyn would come in at 7:55 a.m., say something briefly to him, then excuse herself to go to the restroom.

From there, she would be taken out the back door and directly to Omega HQ. Steve categorically refused to risk her life by having her in the middle of a sting operation.

And the operation was huge. Not only were the dozen employees and customers in the restaurant Omega agents, but there were SWAT agents all around the building, and most of the people outside were theirs too. The lady walking the dog. The jogger a few blocks over whose route happened to go by the café a few times.

Others. All watching the café. Anyone who entered would be tagged: faces captured on camera, fingerprints collected and filed. Anyone who could possibly be the Watcher—so any male under the age of sixty—would be followed and/or tracked.

Steve had decided to use the Watcher's own means against him. Lillian was still playing the waitress. Her petite form belied the fact that she could kill a person in a dozen ways with her tiny bare hands. She would make sure that anyone who could possibly be the Watcher got a transmitter put on him.

It was a complex operation, but complex was what Omega did.

And it was showtime.

He parked his car, trying to make this all as normal as possible, and walked in the front entrance. Lillian greeted him with a perky "Good morning" and told him to sit wherever he wanted to.

He chose the booth near the corner and sat with his back to the wall so he could see the door. Just like he would do in any given restaurant. At least he didn't have to pretend that he wasn't law enforcement.

The place was relatively empty outside the people working for Omega. There was an older couple at one table and a young mother with her toddler at one of the booths. They would all be checked out but none of them were viable suspects.

The building had been thoroughly swept for explosives—at this point Steve didn't put it past the Watcher to just take out the whole place. They'd also been sure to search the closets and attics and crawl spaces. After what happened earlier this year—a psychopath deciding to reside in an agent's attic until the time was right for a kidnapping—they'd all learned their lesson.

Now all Steve could do was wait and watch. And pray that nothing tipped off the Watcher. It wouldn't take much.

Five minutes later a man came in, their first real possible suspect. He was tall, sort of bulky, wearing business attire. Jon's voice came on in Steve's ear.

"We've got him. Got a good shot of his face. Running it now to see if he shows up in any of our facial-recognition software."

"He's got a briefcase," Steve murmured behind his hand.

"Roger that."

A briefcase could carry explosives or a weapon.

"Infrared on the briefcase suggests no explosives," Aidan Killock, SWAT's explosives expert, said through the earpiece. He was in a different van outside.

The man was getting a coffee and muffin to go.

"Tag him anyway, Lillian."

He saw her nod briefly before she came around the counter and stood before the man.

"Here," she said, reaching up and messing with the back of his collar. "That was folded up a little, but now it's perfect."

"Thank you." The man seemed relieved and flattered to have received such attention from someone with Lillian's looks.

And the transmitter in his collar would allow them to track him.

"We've got him," Jon said. "He's not showing up in any of our facial software."

"I don't think that's him. Build isn't right for the guy who came at me on the motorcycle."

But Steve knew they would follow him anyway.

Business began to pick up as a number of people entered, some couples but a few single guys. Steve had to trust his team to do their jobs, because right at 7:55 a.m. Rosalyn walked in the door.

She waved to him and he stood and hugged her as if he hadn't seen her in two days rather than just the hour it had been.

"Are you hungry?" he asked her as they sat down at the booth.

"I'm always hungry."

This, again, was part of the script they had worked out last night. The Watcher had to be listening.

"What do you feel like?"

"Something soft. I have a bad toothache."

Lillian came over and took their order. Steve asked Rosalyn how she was feeling and if the baby had moved again.

He wanted Rosalyn out of there. The more crowded it got in the café, the more tense Steve became.

There were three men in the café right now who could possibly be the Watcher. One in particular looked nervous. But then again, Steve didn't think the Watcher would look nervous.

Something wasn't right.

Steve brought his hand up to his mouth and turned his head to the side. "I'm sending Rosalyn out now."

"Are you sure it's not too soon?" Jon asked.

"I don't care. There are too many unknown variables."

"Roger that. The car is waiting."

Rosalyn didn't have an earpiece in case the transmitter also picked up on what was being said to her.

Steve nodded at her. She nodded back, knowing it was time to go. She reached over and grabbed his hand, squeezing it. He winked at her.

"I've got to go to the restroom."

"Okay."

She stood and walked to the back. The agent in the car reported a few minutes later that he safely had Rosalyn and they were headed back to HQ.

Whatever happened now, at least Rosalyn was safe. He breathed a sigh of relief.

It was short-lived, as a man—the nervous one he saw earlier—sat down in the booth across from him.

He pulled at a gun and pointed it straight at Steve.

"I don't think we've met. I'm the Watcher."

Chapter Twenty-Four

A cascade of emotions flooded Steve.

Rage that this bastard had terrorized Rosalyn for so long. And other women too, to the point of them killing themselves.

Relief that Rosalyn was gone, safe. Out of his clutches. She'd never be in this man's clutches again.

Surprise. This wasn't what he'd thought the Watcher would look like. He wasn't sure exactly what he'd thought the Watcher would look like, but it wasn't unkempt and sweaty like this man. But how did you put a face to a monster?

Either their plan had worked perfectly and the Watcher had grossly underestimated who Steve was and what sort of weight he carried in law enforcement, or the man had nerves of steel. He'd just pulled a gun on a cop in broad daylight with dozens of witnesses.

Or perhaps his intent had always been to kill Steve and he didn't care who saw.

Over the man's shoulder Steve could already see Lillian and the other Omega agents escorting the patrons out of the restaurant.

"Don't let any of them go," Steve said into his communication device. He didn't care if the man across from him knew he had backup. Let him worry.

"We're getting everyone's info. Why don't you worry about the guy pointing a gun at you."

"I'm assuming Ashton has him in his sights."

"Roger that, boss," Ashton's voice came through his ear. "But you'll be scrubbing brain matter off yourself for a long time."

Steve was tempted to tell him to take the shot. He had a gun, was pointing it at Steve, might turn and start shooting innocent people any moment. It would be considered an unfortunate but necessary kill.

Steve wasn't even sure he'd consider it that unfortunate.

But something wasn't right. Since his one sentence introducing himself, the man hadn't said anything. His hands were shaking. He was sweating.

"Nervous?" Steve asked.

The man nodded. "I'm the Watcher."

"Yeah, you said that." Steve took a sip of the cup of coffee Lillian had given him while Rosalyn was here, more to put the other man at ease than anything else. "Don't you have anything else you want to say to me? You know we have the place surrounded, don't you?"

"I am the Watcher." The man was sweating and the gun in his hand was shaking.

"Jon, you got an opinion of what's going on here?"

"Obviously the guy is highly stressed. I don't know, Steve. If I had to guess, I would say this isn't him. But then why is he pointing a gun at you?"

Tears squeezed out of the man's eyes. "I am the Watcher."

Steve gestured to Lillian to come over and plucked a

pen out of her pocket. The Watcher continued to point the gun at Steve, not paying attention to Lillian.

Because he thought she wasn't a threat or for another reason entirely?

Like being given instructions to keep the gun pointed on Steve.

"What's your name?" Steve asked the man.

"I am the Watcher."

"How about I arrest you and we figure out your name once you're in custody."

The gun shook more, but the man didn't pull the trigger.

Steve wrote on the napkin. *Are you being forced?*

He spun the napkin and pushed it over where the man could read it. Tears poured out of the man's eyes as he nodded. He reached up and flipped his collar.

It was a transmitter just like he'd found on Rosalyn's clothes.

The Watcher was using this man as a patsy.

"All right, look, let's just talk this out. Okay?"

The man nodded that he understood. Steve wrote on the napkin. *Can he see you?*

The man shook his head no. Steve gestured for him to put down the gun. After a few moments he did so.

"You know I'm police, right?"

"I am the Watcher."

Evidently that was all the man was allowed to say. Steve grabbed another napkin. *Where is the man who did this?*

At my house. Will kill my wife and kids.

"Look, just put the gun down. It's me you want. I don't want anyone else to get hurt by accident." *Address?*

The man wrote it. Then, *I have to kill you or he will kill them.*

Jon's voice sounded in his ear. "I've got the address, Steve, and we have agents en route to the guy's house. They'll go in silently."

Steve picked up the gun and handed it to Lillian.

"You have to put the gun down. If you were going to shoot me, you would've done it by—"

Lillian shot the gun over his head into the wall.

"Oh my God, that guy just shot that guy. He's got a gun!" she screamed at the top of her voice.

"Hey, he's running away—" Derek yelled out, helping along the charade.

Steve reached out and grabbed the transmitter from the guy's collar. He dropped it to the ground and stomped on it.

"Any others?" he mouthed.

The man shook his head, confusion plain in his eyes.

"We've got law enforcement en route to your house," Steve told the man. "What's your name?"

"Donny Showalter. He told me I had to come in here and shoot you. He told me all I could say was that we hadn't met and that I was the Watcher." The guy put his face in his hands. "I have to get to my house."

"How far do you live from here?"

"Only a few blocks."

"Steve, our agents are there," Jon told him. "We have eyes inside. The family is tied up but no one is hurt."

He relayed the information to the man, who promptly deflated on the table in relief.

"Is anybody there with them?" Steve waited for the information to be relayed back to him.

A few minutes later Jon was back in his ear. "Steve, the wife says the guy who tied them up left right after Donny did."

He'd been around here. Maybe in the coffeehouse or directly outside. Seeing what happened. Probably hoping they would kill Donny and cause even more chaos.

"Is my family really okay? I need to see them."

"I'll have them call you in just a minute, okay?"

Donny nodded.

"Can you tell me anything about the man who put you up to this? What he looked like?"

"No. He broke into our house this morning while we were having breakfast. He was wearing a mask."

Damn it. The Watcher had been smarter than they thought. He'd been making sure this wasn't a setup, and if he was anywhere in the vicinity, he would know that Steve was much more deeply entrenched in law enforcement than just some sort of beat cop.

Taking him by surprise was no longer an option.

"Steve." Jon's voice was more somber than he'd ever heard it.

"Go, Jon." He pressed the earpiece farther in his ear so he could hear over the chaos going on around him.

"I just got word from HQ. Travis Loveridge and Rosalyn never checked in. They found the car about a half mile from HQ. Loveridge is dead. Rosalyn is missing."

ROSALYN HAD AGENT Loveridge's blood all over her. Her arms, her neck, her hands. She couldn't get it off.

Of course, dried blood was the least of her problems.

She stared at the man driving the car. "I remember

you. You're Lindsey's psychologist from when she was a teenager. Dr. Zinger."

"Zenger." He turned and smiled at her. Like they were old friends or something. Like he hadn't walked up to the car while they were stopped at a red light and shot the agent driving. Like he hadn't been stalking and terrorizing her for the better part of a year.

Rosalyn shrank back against the car door. He hadn't touched her at all, except to catch her when he drugged her and tied her hands, but she didn't want to take a chance.

She was barely holding it together. If he touched her, she might start screaming and never stop.

"Lindsey liked you," she whispered. "Thought you were so handsome."

Rosalyn remembered. They'd been eighteen. Lindsey had been in trouble again and sent to group counseling this time. When Rosalyn had come home from college for a semester break, she'd asked her sister how things were going.

Rosalyn hadn't been encouraged when all her sister would talk about was how hot the counselor was rather than showing any interest in truly kicking her drug habit.

He was handsome, if Rosalyn could distance herself enough from the terror. Clean-cut, short brown hair. Good physique. But all Rosalyn saw was the monster.

"You killed her," Rosalyn whispered.

He shrugged, not looking at her. "If it helps, she never knew it was me."

It didn't help at all.

Rosalyn's hands were tied with some sort of zip tie. "Where are you taking me?"

"We have to get out of Colorado, of course. Your boyfriend is already dead—I sent a friend of mine in to shoot him. Since Steve didn't know who I was, I'm sure he won't care that it wasn't me who actually killed him."

Rosalyn stared and could hear her breath sawing in and out of her nose and mouth. Was he telling the truth? Was Steve really dead?

"I wasn't exactly sure how the whole café scenario was going to play out. But when I saw you leave out the back door, I knew it had been some sort of setup. How did you know I would be there?"

Rosalyn tried to get her panic under control. She had to keep the fact that Omega Sector was onto him a secret. "We didn't. I guess Steve was doing stuff just in case. I was hitching a ride from that guy to the bus station. You didn't have to kill him."

Zenger's eyes were narrowed as he turned to look at her. She wasn't sure if he was buying her story. "Hitch-hiking is dangerous."

She bit back a hysterical laugh. "Ended up being much more dangerous for him."

She looked out the window again. They were on the interstate. There was no way she could jump out of the car now and survive.

She refused to believe him when he said Steve was dead. Zenger hadn't been there; he'd been too busy killing that poor agent who'd been with her. There was no way he could know for sure Steve had actually died. Maybe the shot hadn't killed him.

Steve was alive and would be coming for her. He and

Jon and Brandon...they would figure out who Zenger was; they would find him.

Steve would rescue her. He wouldn't leave her and the baby in the hands of this madman.

She had to hold on to that or there was no way she would survive.

They sat in silence for miles.

"Where are we going?" she asked again finally.

"Back to familiar ground. I'm from Mobile too, you know. I have a nice little place where you can stay."

"And do what?" She couldn't keep the revulsion out of her voice, not that she tried.

He laughed, a friendly sound under any other circumstances. "Rosalyn, I'm not like that at all. I don't plan to force myself on you in any way. That's beneath me."

"But killing people isn't?"

He sighed. "I don't kill out of choice or some sort of sport. Honestly. It brings me no pleasure."

"Then why kill at all?"

"For the research. This is all for science, Rosalyn."

Oh God, Jon and Brandon had been right all along with their profile. That gave Rosalyn hope that they would be able to follow through and find her.

"Science?"

"I am a psychologist. I help people. The data I'm collecting about isolation will be used to help disturbed people for decades to come."

He honestly believed it.

"Isolation?"

"Yes, yes, that's what all of this has been about. I take young women and divide them from everyone in their life. I prey upon their worst fears and then see what they do to cope. How long they can last."

She wondered if he would tell her, if she asked, about the tracking devices. About the dentist and the one in her tooth. But she didn't want to tip her hand.

"What happens to them when they can't last any longer?"

Zenger shook his head sadly. "Unfortunately, they commit suicide. It's a regrettable side effect of this research. But don't you understand? The loss is acceptable for the greater good. I am on the forefront of research that every mental-health-care professional would love to be a part of."

If it hadn't been absolutely sickening, Zenger's zeal for his work would almost have been commendable.

"Was that what you wanted with me? For me to kill myself?"

"You, my dear, you have been the longest-lasting subject in my research." He glanced at her again. "And to think, you weren't supposed to be my original subject."

"Lindsey was."

"Exactly. But I realized that the drug abuse made Lindsey a poor test subject. You were much stronger, more resilient. I just had to wait for the right time."

She assumed that meant wait until she went to the dentist. The dentist that Lindsey had suggested. Had suggested because a doctor mentioned it to her.

Zenger had been that doctor. Had helped orchestrate the entire thing from the beginning.

"I'm sure your pregnancy has played an important

role in your resilience. You don't want to die. You want to live for your baby."

Maybe she could get him to understand that. Make him think that she could understand the importance of his research so he would let her go.

"Yes. The baby is an unforeseen variable with me, I'm sure." Rosalyn nodded. "It must mean I can't fit into the conceived categories and corrupt your data analysis."

He nodded, obviously glad she understood. "I forgot you majored in accounting. So you are familiar with data and experimentation."

"Yes. You're obviously the expert, but I do have some knowledge. I know the baby changes things."

"You're absolutely right. He does. I had to really think about what needed to be done when I found out you were pregnant."

"Dr. Zenger, now that you've explained it to me, I see how important your research is. Like you said, the baby changes things for me. I can never be truly isolated from people when I have a little person growing inside me."

"That's exactly right, Rosalyn. I'm so happy you understand."

"So you'll let me go? You know I will never tell anyone about your research. Unless you want me to, of course."

She meant it with every fiber of her being. If she could get out of this with both her and the baby unharmed, she would do whatever Zenger wanted.

Steve would hunt him down to the ends of the earth, but Rosalyn would stay out of it.

"No, I can't let you go, Rosalyn. I'm sorry."

She tried not to let the disappointment crush her. She needed to reason with him. "But what about the baby? Like you said, I don't fit any categories anymore. I'm not useful for your research."

"Rosalyn, you were an outlier even before the baby. I'm not sure you would've ever been statistically useful."

"Then why are you taking me to Mobile?"

"I'll keep you there until you have the baby. Then, unfortunately, I'll have to kill you. Like you said, you're not useful for my research anymore."

"What about the baby?"

"Oh, he will give me a lifetime worth of data. Just think of what I'll be able to do."

Suddenly there wasn't enough air in the car. Rosalyn reached for the handle of the door. She didn't care that they were on the interstate. She couldn't stay in this car a moment longer. She would have to take her chances with jumping.

Zenger swung the car toward the shoulder, slowing rapidly, grabbing her arm tightly to keep her from jumping out.

She fought him. Slowing was what she wanted him to do. It gave her a better chance to survive.

"Stop, Rosalyn."

She kept fighting.

He pulled the car to a stop, both of them slamming forward as he hit the brakes hard. Now he had both hands to hold her with.

She didn't care if she had to stay here and fight him for the rest of her life. She was not going to let him drive her somewhere where he could keep her baby and do experiments on him.

She felt a sharp sting on the side of her neck. It took only a few moments before all her movements began to feel slushy.

"No..." she whispered. She felt tears leak out of her eyes, but her arms were too heavy to wipe them.

"You fought the good fight. Now go to sleep."

She tried not to, but in just moments the darkness pulled her under.

Chapter Twenty-Five

Steve did what he did best: worked the problem.

He did not focus on the fact a psychopath had Rosalyn in his clutches. Did not focus on the fact that they had no idea where said psychopath was taking her or how they would find her. That they still had no idea what the Watcher looked like or where he was from.

Because if he focused on those things, the fear and agony would overwhelm him.

He'd known helplessness when Melanie had died; it had ripped a hole in his heart.

But he knew he wouldn't survive if Rosalyn didn't make it.

He kept that all pushed aside because it would do nothing to help them find her now.

Travis Loveridge was dead. Evidently the Watcher had walked up to their car while they were stopped at a red light and shot him point-blank in the head. There had been witnesses, but no one had been able to see the Watcher's face. They'd seen him pick up a woman—an unconscious woman with long black hair—and carry her to his car parked at the side of the street.

A gray sedan. There were thousands of them on the roads. They were checking, but so far a dead end.

They'd pulled up the feed from the traffic camera, but it had been pointing in the wrong direction. Another dead end.

Brandon was interviewing Gavin from the café and his wife. Molly's lab crew was checking for forensics at the house. But so far...

Steve was studying computerized maps. Working on the assumption that the Watcher was taking Rosalyn out of Colorado. He assumed back to Mobile.

But it was too far to make it in one day. Steve knew from personal experience a week ago going the opposite way. He had every Omega person who could be spared making calls to hotels along the interstate heading south.

Steve personally had called the state and highway patrols for New Mexico, Kansas and Texas. He wanted them to understand the direness of the situation; he didn't want it to be just be another report that came across their desks.

It was all long shots, but Steve would keep taking long shots until one of them paid off. It was getting late now. Dark. The thought of her alone with the Watcher overnight...

Derek put a hand on Steve's shoulder. "How are you holding up?"

Steve wiped a hand across his face. What could he say?

That panic was crawling up his spine, threatening to take over not only his whole body but the whole world?

How would anyone understand that?

"She's alive, Steve. When the panic starts to overwhelm you, you push it back down with the thought that until we know definitely otherwise, Rosalyn and the baby are both alive."

Maybe someone could understand that.

Derek could. Hadn't Steve seen the very agony in his own eyes in Derek's eighteen months ago when a sadistic bastard had kidnapped Molly?

Derek had moved heaven and earth to get her back. Steve had helped. He prayed he would get his own happily-ever-after with Rosalyn and their child.

"I thought she was dead once, Derek. And that was before I knew what she meant to me. I'll be damned if I'll let her die again not knowing I love her."

Molly walked through the door. "You're not going to have to."

Both men turned to her. "What do you mean?"

"I've found the frequency the Watcher was using to track Rosalyn from a transmitter Jon and Brandon brought back from other victims. The transmitters were still live."

"What?" Derek asked.

"I don't know if the Watcher was trying to keep tabs on the families or what. But I was able to use them to find other transmitters. Actually, I've found *all* the women—since he used the same frequency for all the transmitters."

"How do we know which one is Rosalyn?"

She ran over to the computer and brought up a navigation system on the screen.

"I'm going to assume she's the one halfway between

here and Mobile." She pointed to a red dot near Oklahoma City.

Oklahoma City was less than six hundred miles. They could've made it there if the Watcher drove at a rapid pace.

He would've been moving at a rapid pace.

Derek kissed Molly and ran for the door. "The team and I will meet you at the helicopter in ten minutes," he called back to Steve.

Molly touched Steve's arm as he moved toward the door and handed him a small GPS screen. "You're going to need this. Outside Oklahoma City is the best I can do from this far away. As you get closer, this monitor will provide more details."

Steve kissed her forehead. "Thank you, Molly."

She shrugged. "You once broke all the rules and gave Derek a plane to come after me. If you hadn't, I wouldn't be here now." She pushed him. "Go get your girl."

TRUE TO MOLLY'S WORD, the GPS continued to become more detailed the closer they got to Oklahoma.

The transmission wasn't in Oklahoma City at all; it was in Guymon, a much smaller town northwest of the city.

At some point the Watcher had gotten off the main interstates, which had been a smart move on his part.

"Boss, there's no actual helicopter landing site big enough for us in Guymon. But we've been given permission to land on the high school field." Lillian was flying the helicopter. One of her many skills.

"Good." Steve spoke into the headset he and the five members of the SWAT team were wearing.

As they got closer, Steve was able to pinpoint Rosalyn's location. A hotel about two miles south of the high school. Steve provided the info to Lillian, who relayed it to the local police, who would also be providing them transportation to the hotel. They landed a few minutes later.

The local deputies were there with a county van to take the SWAT team and Steve to the location. Steve could tell the team was ready.

There wasn't anybody he would want at his back more than these men—and this woman—right here.

"You guys…" He looked at Derek, then at Lillian. He needed to express how important Rosalyn was to him.

"No need to say it, boss," Derek told him. "We'll get her out, safely."

They were less than a minute out when the news came over the van's CB unit.

"We've got reports of shots fired at the Best Holiday hotel on Thirty-Second Street."

That was the hotel where Rosalyn's tracker had stopped.

Steve's curse was foul. The van squealed into the hotel parking lot and Steve and the team poured out the back door before it even stopped moving.

The place was surrounded by cop cars, officers using their vehicles for cover, weapons drawn.

Steve rushed up to the officer in charge, a kid, probably in his mid-twenties. Doubtful he had any experience with this sort of situation. "I'm Steve Drackett, head of the Critical Response Division of Omega Sector. I need your name and a rundown of the situation."

"Keith Holloway, sir. Evidently a man was bringing in his exhausted pregnant wife, who'd been very sick. He was half carrying her, according to one witness. But then she started screaming that he was kidnapping her and he pulled out a gun. Shot the clerk."

"How long have you been out here?" he asked Holloway.

"Less than two minutes, sir."

Steve looked over at Ashton. "Got any ideas for a distance shot?"

Ashton was already putting his distance scope on his rifle. "It will be hard without knowing where Rosalyn is."

"I'm going in to draw him out. As soon as you can get a good shot, you take it."

"Steve—" Derek put an arm out as Steve stood up.

"He's trapped. He knows it. Getting out with Rosalyn will be nearly impossible. He'll cut his losses and shoot her as a distraction. And he knows the longer he stays, the less chance he'll have to get away."

"He'll shoot you."

The other members of the team were taking out their rifles too. None of them were as good a shot as Ashton, but that didn't matter now.

Steve looked at them. "I'll draw him out. You take him down."

Mind made up, he walked quickly to the front door and went through. A little bell chimed as he did.

"Leave right now or I will kill her!" Steve couldn't see anyone but could tell they were behind the counter.

"I think it's time we meet face-to-face, Watcher."

He heard Rosalyn's sob but didn't know if it was from pain or relief.

"Who are you?"

"You sent someone to kill me today. That didn't work out."

"Steve Drackett? How did you find me?" His tone was incredulous.

Steve took another step closer. He needed to draw the man out. "The same way you've been finding Rosalyn all these months. And the other women. We know about the transmitters in the teeth. It's over."

"Do you know what you've done?" He stood up now but kept Rosalyn right in front of him, his gun to her head. No one would be able to get a clean shot.

And Rosalyn was glassy-eyed, pale and covered in blood. The Watcher seemed to be half propping her up.

Steve forced himself to stay focused.

"You've ruined my research. My life's work! You have no idea what good I was doing for the world." He was frantic, voice high-pitched, hysterical.

"All I want is Rosalyn." Steve kept his arms out in front of him but shifted his weight to the balls of his feet. He was going to make a move that would draw the Watcher's attention and gun to him.

"No. She's already promised me her baby. She understands my research and knows how important it is."

Now. He had to do it now.

But Rosalyn beat him to it. Her eyes rolled up in the back of her head and she slid to the floor.

The Watcher couldn't hold her up and turned his gun on Steve.

Glass shattered all around him and the Watcher flew back and onto the ground, dead, shot six times. Every single member of the SWAT team had taken him out.

Steve jumped over the desk counter and picked up Rosalyn's still form. There was more blood on her now. Had she been shot? His hands were so shaky he couldn't get a pulse.

Derek and Lillian made their way to him first. He was rocking Rosalyn in his arms but couldn't get her to wake up.

"She's bleeding," he told Derek. "She's hurt."

Lillian put two fingers at Rosalyn's throat. "She's alive, Steve. I think she's been drugged."

All he could see was the blood. "But she's bleeding."

He felt Derek's hand on his shoulder, pressing hard.

"You're bleeding, boss. Bastard got a shot off at you before we took him down."

Steve didn't care. As long as Rosalyn was alive, the baby was okay, Steve didn't care about himself. He pulled her close to him, uncaring of the pain, certain he was never going to let her go ever again.

Chapter Twenty-Six

"You're going to get fired if you keep taking all this time off work, you know," Rosalyn told Steve as they walked through the sands of Pensacola beach a month later.

He smiled at her and pulled her closer to his side. "I have ten years' worth of vacation time saved up. I'm not going to get fired."

"So you brought me back here to the scene of the crime, literally and figuratively."

She was glad. The drugs Zenger had given her had slowed both her and the baby's heart rates to dangerously low levels. She'd been unconscious for two days. But that had probably been for the best since Steve had been shot while rescuing her.

He'd gone into surgery and they'd removed the bullet, but there had been some pretty significant damage done to his shoulder. It would require quite a bit of rehab to get it back to full motion again.

While she was unconscious, since the drug Zenger gave her worked similarly to a general anesthetic, Steve had convinced the doctor of the medical necessity of having the crown with the transmitter removed and replaced with just a plain old regular crown.

Rosalyn had been thrilled to hear it, even though the Watcher was dead and it didn't matter anymore.

The Watcher was truly gone. Rosalyn had explained who he was, and with the technology Molly had cracked, they had let the other women know what had happened to them so they could get the transmitters removed.

Of course, it was too late for the four women they knew of who had committed suicide and a fifth one whose case they hadn't discovered yet.

But Rosalyn had made it. She was still so thankful she'd met Steve at this beach—now seven months ago—because otherwise she wasn't sure that she would've.

He was everything to her.

Rosalyn had been alone most of her life, even when she'd been surrounded by her family. This past month she'd been shown what a family was really meant to be. People willing to stand with you, protect you, put their lives on the line for you.

Family was something that had nothing to do with blood and DNA and everything to do with love. She knew no matter what happened between her and Steve, the baby she carried would have a family who loved him. The people in Omega already did.

She knew Steve loved the baby. She just wished she knew how he felt about *her*. Even though she'd lived in his house the last month, they still hadn't talked about the future.

"I'm not really good at romance," he murmured.

She shook her head. "Says the man taking me on a stroll on the beach as the sun is setting. I think you're doing okay."

"There's something I've been wanting to ask you since the first night we met."

"Oh yeah, what's that?"

"Will you have dinner with me?"

"What?" She laughed.

"I want to take you out to dinner and on dates. I want to court you and show you how much you mean to me. I want to show you that you can trust me with your secrets. You can trust me with your heart."

"Steve, if this is about the baby…"

"No." He turned so they were face-to-face. "All of that has nothing to do with the baby. It's what I've wanted to say to you since the first minute you walked into that tiki bar when I could tell you were capital-*T* trouble."

He smiled at her. "I'm excited and terrified about the baby, as all new fathers should be. But you're the one I want, Rosalyn. Always. I will ask you to marry me tomorrow. But today, I just want to take you out. Will you have dinner with me?"

She reached her arms around his waist and pulled him to her.

"Yes. To both."

And right there in the sand where everything had almost ended, her new life began.

* * * * *

*Look for more Omega stories
from Janie Crouch in 2017.*

*You'll find them wherever
Harlequin Intrigue books are sold!*

COMING NEXT MONTH FROM

⊞ HARLEQUIN®

INTRIGUE

Available January 17, 2017

#1689 LAW AND DISORDER
The Finnegan Connection • by Heather Graham
Dakota "Kody" Cameron never expected to be taken hostage in her historic Florida manor, especially not by men disguised as old-time gangsters searching for a fortune hidden somewhere on the grounds. Among them is undercover FBI agent Nick Connolly, who must protect Kody before she recognizes him from their shared past and compromises his cover.

#1690 HOT COMBAT
Ballistic Cowboys • by Elle James
Working for Homeland Security brings John "Ghost" Caspar home to Wyoming, far from the combat he knew as an elite Navy SEAL. Charlie McClain let go of her old flame years ago, and has been raising her daughter and tracking terrorist threats online—until her anonymity is compromised. Now reunited, Ghost will stop at nothing to keep Charlie and her daughter safe.

#1691 TEXAS-SIZED TROUBLE
Cattlemen Crime Club • by Barb Han
The O'Briens and the McCabes have a deep rivalry and get on like fire and gasoline. So when Faith McCabe's secret affair with Ryder O'Brien results in pregnancy, she keeps the baby secret and walks away. But when her half brother goes missing, Faith knows there's only one man she can turn to.

#1692 EAGLE WARRIOR
Apache Protectors: Tribal Thunder • by Jenna Kernan
Turquoise Guardian Ray Strong isn't sure how he's going to protect Morgan Hooke when he can't take her word about missing blood money for a killer her father took down. But when the young mother is targeted by an ecoextremist group, Ray realizes that Morgan may have more than clues to the missing money—she may know the identity of the extremists who paid her father.

#1693 MOUNTAIN WITNESS
Tennessee SWAT • by Lena Diaz
Julie Webb came back to Destiny, Tennessee, to get away from her estranged husband and family after an unspeakable betrayal. And maybe it's destiny that her new neighbor is Chris Downing, a police detective and part-time SWAT officer, because it's going to take all his skills to protect her when darkness from her past resurfaces.

#1694 WILD MONTANA • by Danica Winters
Both Agent Casper Lawrence and park ranger Alexis Finch know how it feels when love goes wrong. But when a grisly murder unveils a dark conspiracy in Glacier National Park, they can't fight their feelings any more than they can see just how deep the investigation will go before the truth comes to light.

YOU CAN FIND MORE INFORMATION ON UPCOMING HARLEQUIN® TITLES, FREE EXCERPTS AND MORE AT WWW.HARLEQUIN.COM.

HICNM0117

REQUEST YOUR FREE BOOKS!
2 FREE NOVELS PLUS 2 FREE GIFTS!

⊞ HARLEQUIN®

I N T R I G U E

BREATHTAKING ROMANTIC SUSPENSE

YES! Please send me 2 FREE Harlequin® Intrigue novels and my 2 FREE gifts (gifts are worth about $10). After receiving them, if I don't wish to receive any more books, I can return the shipping statement marked "cancel." If I don't cancel, I will receive 6 brand-new novels every month and be billed just $4.74 per book in the U.S. or $5.49 per book in Canada. That's a savings of at least 12% off the cover price! It's quite a bargain! Shipping and handling is just 50¢ per book in the U.S. and 75¢ per book in Canada.* I understand that accepting the 2 free books and gifts places me under no obligation to buy anything. I can always return a shipment and cancel at any time. Even if I never buy another book, the two free books and gifts are mine to keep forever.

182/382 HDN GH3D

Name _____ (PLEASE PRINT)

Address _____ Apt. #

City _____ State/Prov. _____ Zip/Postal Code

Signature (if under 18, a parent or guardian must sign)

Mail to the Reader Service:
IN U.S.A.: P.O. Box 1867, Buffalo, NY 14240-1867
IN CANADA: P.O. Box 609, Fort Erie, Ontario L2A 5X3

**Are you a subscriber to Harlequin® Intrigue books
and want to receive the larger-print edition?
Call 1-800-873-8635 or visit www.ReaderService.com.**

* Terms and prices subject to change without notice. Prices do not include applicable taxes. Sales tax applicable in N.Y. Canadian residents will be charged applicable taxes. Offer not valid in Quebec. This offer is limited to one order per household. Not valid for current subscribers to Harlequin Intrigue books. All orders subject to credit approval. Credit or debit balances in a customer's account(s) may be offset by any other outstanding balance owed by or to the customer. Please allow 4 to 6 weeks for delivery. Offer available while quantities last.

Your Privacy—The Reader Service is committed to protecting your privacy. Our Privacy Policy is available online at www.ReaderService.com or upon request from the Reader Service.

We make a portion of our mailing list available to reputable third parties that offer products we believe may interest you. If you prefer that we not exchange your name with third parties, or if you wish to clarify or modify your communication preferences, please visit us at www.ReaderService.com/consumerchoice or write to us at Reader Service Preference Service, P.O. Box 9062, Buffalo, NY 14240-9062. Include your complete name and address.

HI15

Nick and Kody Cameron had passed briefly, like
proverbial ships in the night, but he hadn't had the least
problem recognizing her today. He knew her, because
they had both paused to stare at one another at the pub.

Instant attraction? Definitely on his part, and he could
have sworn on hers, too.

If Dakota Cameron saw his face, if she gave any
indication that she knew him, and knew that he was an
FBI man…

They'd both be dead.

And it didn't help the situation that she was battle
ready—ready to lay down her life for her friends.

Then again, there should have been a way for him to
stop this. If it hadn't been for the little boy who had been
taken…

Kody Cameron had a ledger opened before her, but she
was looking at him. Quizzically.

It seemed as if she suspected she knew him but couldn't figure out from where.

"You're not as crazy as the others," she said softly. "I can sense that about you. But you need to do something to stop this. That treasure he's talking about has been missing for years and years. God knows, maybe it's in the Everglades, swallowed up in a sinkhole. You don't want to be a part of this—I know you don't. And those guys are lethal. They'll hurt someone…kill someone. This is still a death-penalty state, you know. Please, if you would just—"

He found himself walking over to her at the desk and replying in a heated whisper, "Just do what he says and find the damned treasure. Lie if you have to! Find something that will make Dillinger believe that you know where the treasure is. Give him a damned map to find it. He won't think twice about killing people, but he won't kill just for the hell of it. Don't give him a reason."

"You're not one of them. You have to stop this. Get away from them," she said.

She was beautiful, earnest, passionate. He wanted to reassure her. To rip off his mask and tell her that law enforcement was on it all.

But that was impossible, lest they all die quickly.

He had to keep his distance and keep her, the kidnapped child and the others in the house alive.

Don't miss LAW AND DISORDER
by New York Times *bestselling author Heather Graham,*
available February 2017 wherever
Harlequin® Intrigue books and ebooks are sold.

www.Harlequin.com

HIEXP0117

THE WORLD IS BETTER WITH

Romance

Harlequin has everything from contemporary, passionate and heartwarming to suspenseful and inspirational stories.

Whatever your mood, we have a romance just for you!

Connect with us to find your next great read, special offers and more.

f /HarlequinBooks

🐦 @HarlequinBooks

www.HarlequinBlog.com

www.Harlequin.com/Newsletters